THE
ROCK OF IVANORE

Book One of The Celestine Chronicles

by
Laurisa White Reyes

Tanglewood • Terre Haute, IN

Published by Tanglewood Publishing, Inc., May, 2012.
Text © Laurisa White Reyes 2012

Cover art by Tristan Elwell & interior art by Kathleen Everts
Design by Amy Alick Perich

Tanglewood Publishing, Inc.
4400 Hulman Street
Terre Haute, IN 47803
www.tanglewoodbooks.com

Printed by Maple-Vail Press, York, PA, USA
10 9 8 7 6 5 4 3 2 1

ISBN-13 978-1-933718-60-6
ISBN-10 1-933718-60-9

Library of Congress Cataloging-in-Publication Data

Reyes, Laurisa White.
    The Rock of Ivanore / Laurisa White Reyes.
        p. cm.
    Summary: The annual Great Quest announced by the wizard Zyll requires Marcus and other boys of the village who are coming of age to find the Rock of Ivanore without knowing what it is or where it can be found, but unless they develop new powers of magic and find strength to survive wild lands and fierce enemies, they will lose their honor and live menial lives of shame.
    ISBN 978-1-933718-60-6 (hardback) -- ISBN 1-933718-60-9 ()
    [1. Adventure and adventurers--Fiction. 2. Magic--Fiction. 3. Coming of age--Fiction. 4. Wizards--Fiction. 5. Fantasy.] I. Title.
    PZ7.R3303Roc 2012
    [Fic]--dc23
                                2011039335

For my son,
Marcum,
for whom this story was born.

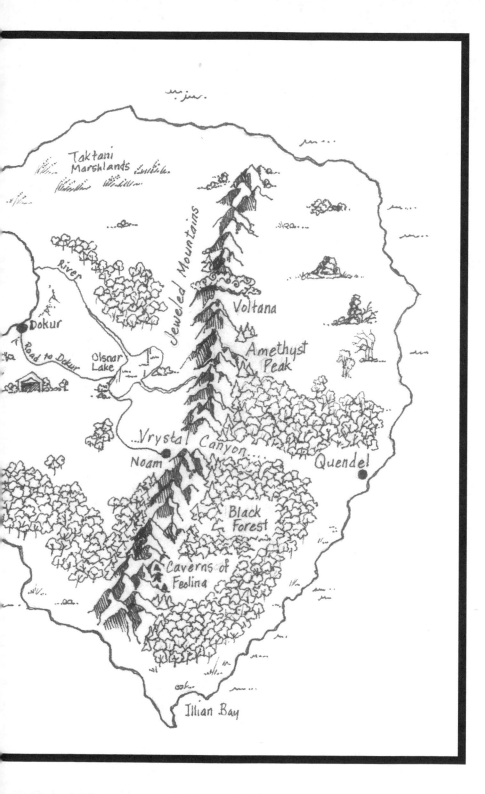

Prologue

The old enchanter rose from his cot, his joints creaking like rusty hinges. His sleep had been troubled, and thoughts of the days ahead worried him. Taking care not to wake his apprentice, Zyll went to the table in the center of the room, though his legs were so stiff that even traveling the width of his cottage required the use of a walking stick. With his free hand, he took a copper bowl down from a shelf and set it on the table. He grinned at the fresh bucket of water on the hearth, grateful that the boy had remembered to fill it this time.

Zyll ladled water into the bowl and peered at his reflection in it. How changed he looked, how unlike the man he used to be. His hair, once thick and dark, had thinned and grown white, and the skin around his mouth had creased. But his eyes still glowed with the vibrancy of youth. One thing, at least, had remained the same.

He laid his walking stick across the table and leaned closer to better view the image before him. The water darkened, and another face replaced Zyll's reflection, a younger man not altogether human—a half-breed.

The image widened. Crouching in a dark corridor, the half-breed crept from shadow to shadow. Slipping past two sentries, he entered a small chapel. He hurried to the altar and released a hidden latch that opened a small door near its base. Zyll watched as the half-breed removed a scroll concealed within and hid it beneath his cloak.

Just then, the chapel door flew open with a tremendous shudder. There, framed in torchlight, stood a man with red hair accompanied by seven manlike beasts with hairy faces pocked with repulsive scars. The redheaded man charged angrily into the room, his sword slashing down in a wide, rapid arc. The half-breed hastily drew his sword just in time to deflect the blow and countered with his own. His blade tasted flesh, and the redheaded man collapsed to his knees, his hands grasping the side of his bloody face.

The half-breed spied a small object on the floor and managed to snatch it up before the beasts attacked. Though he fought them with inhuman strength, they soon drove him up against the wall.

Cornered and outnumbered, the half-breed turned to the window and gazed down. The image in the bowl shifted, and Zyll saw what the half-breed saw: angry ocean waves beating against the rocks far below. Suddenly the waves rushed up toward him, and Zyll realized that the half-breed had leapt from the window. Zyll watched him fall, and as he fell, the half-breed twisted his body to look up at the sky. For one fleeting moment before he plunged into the sea, his inhuman cat eyes met Zyll's.

The enchanter's breath caught in his throat, and he stumbled back. When he looked in the bowl again, the image had vanished. Zyll dropped into a chair, resting his weary arms on the table. He glanced at the fair-haired boy who slept on, then choked out a whisper. "So it begins."

THE QUEST BEGINS

One

The morning of Marcus Frye's fourteenth birthday may have seemed ordinary to some, but for him no day had ever dawned brighter. The birds' songs sounded sweeter. In the distance, Amethyst Peak looked more brilliant than ever before. Even Master Zyll appeared younger and more spry than usual.

From his cot in the corner of the cottage, Marcus watched the enchanter arrange a pile of wood on the hearth. Zyll inspected his work through a pair of spectacles and nodded with satisfaction. "You are awake," he said, removing his spectacles and wiping them with the sleeve of his robe. "I was beginning to think someone had put a sleeping spell on you."

Marcus arose and went to the table, where a steaming bowl of porridge waited. A clean tunic and trousers lay across the back of a chair.

"Why didn't you wake me to get the wood?" asked Marcus. "The morning air isn't good for you."

"Nonsense," replied Zyll, lowering himself into a chair beside the hearth. An old leather satchel lay in his lap. "Now sit and eat."

Marcus dressed in the clean clothes and sat down. He picked at his breakfast, his stomach too much in knots for food. He preferred instead to watch Zyll mend the satchel, which looked as though it could not withstand one more day's wear. When he had finished, Zyll held the satchel by the shoulder strap and gave it a good hard shake. Its contents, which included a week's worth of bread and dried goat's meat, as well as a few coins and an iron pot, collided with a dull thud. Marcus winced at the thought of finding crumbs for his supper rather than bread.

"There it is now," said Zyll.

Marcus eyed it disdainfully. "Master, the other boys have new satchels. Couldn't we buy one as well?"

"What for?" Zyll replied, handing Marcus the battered satchel. "This bag holds as much as a new one." Then he rose with some effort from his chair to begin filling a kettle with vegetables.

Marcus hesitated making any further requests. He did not want to appear greedy, but this day was special, so he spoke before his courage could leave him. "Master, what about the other supplies?"

"What supplies?" asked Zyll, not looking up from the kettle.

"Well, I'll need a weapon, for one thing."

Zyll tossed the last of the onions into the pot and added some water. "You've no need of weapons, boy. Haven't I taught you well enough how to fend for yourself?"

Marcus thought of the many lessons Zyll had taught him. He had learned the ways of the mystic, and also a bit of history, mathematics, and philosophy. Zyll disapproved of sword fighting but had allowed him to practice with the other boys in the village.

"I'm good with a sword," Marcus reminded him, "but I'm a terrible magician."

Zyll turned toward him. His face held the same pensive expression it always did. "Why do you doubt your abilities?" he asked. "You know magic is nothing more than the art of rearranging the elements that lay before you. Take the logs for instance," he continued. "What is fire but heat? Heat is found in rays of sunlight and in all living things."

Zyll lifted his hand toward the window where a stream of light filtered into the cottage. "We must harvest it from the sunshine, the trees, our own bodies." He lowered his hand, drawing it across Marcus's shoulders. "Compress it to a fine point, direct it toward the logs, and . . ."

With a quick snap of his wrist, the logs burst into flames. Zyll set the kettle over the fire. "This soup will be ready for my afternoon meal."

"I would still prefer a sword," said Marcus.

Zyll's voice was calm yet insistent. "Use your knowledge to obtain those things you need and to defend yourself and others from harm." He doused the fire with a mumbled incantation. Then gesturing toward the hearth, he added, "Give it a try."

Marcus preferred to do his chores without magic, yet he would not refuse his master's request. Turning to the hearth, he focused his attention on the wood and formed an image of brilliant, orange flame in his mind.

"Ignite!" he commanded. He held his breath as he waited for the flames to appear, but nothing happened. "I can't do it!" he said with disgust. "Maybe I shouldn't go on the quest. I know I'll fail."

Zyll studied his apprentice with tender, gray eyes. Marcus knew those eyes well. He had seen them every day of his life. Orphaned at birth, Marcus had been in Zyll's care for as long as he could remember. He was a good master, kind and generous, yet firm. They made a fine pair, he and Zyll, and Marcus imagined no one could have been a better father to him.

When the town council had agreed to let Marcus, a mere orphan, join this year's *Bleôth Camr⁻u*—or, translated from the ancient tongue, "Great Quest"—he was determined to finally prove he was destined for more than servitude.

Every year on the first day of spring, all the boys in Quendel who had reached the age of manhood during the previous year set out on a journey across Imaness. Their purpose: to accomplish some task or retrieve an object as determined by the village elders. The quests were never

easy, often lasting days or even weeks on end. Those who
returned triumphant were bestowed with the most honorable jobs in the village. Those who failed were relegated
to the more mundane positions in life. At first, Marcus
was elated at the news that he would be allowed to par-
ticipate. But now the thought of disappointing Zyll filled
Marcus with shame.

Zyll went to his bookshelf, but he was not interested
in the books. Instead he reached for a wooden chest,
which he carried to the table and raised the lid. After sifting through its contents, he lifted something in his hand.
Though Marcus could not tell what it was, the item was
small enough to be hidden by the old man's fingers.

Zyll turned his gaze on Marcus, though his eyes
seemed to look right through him. With a shake of his
head he remembered the task at hand and laid the object
back inside the chest. After more sifting and searching,
Zyll withdrew another small object and slammed the lid
shut, sending a billow of dust into the air.

"I have not yet given you a gift for your birthday," said
Zyll, holding out his palm. A small metal object lay across it.

"A key?" asked Marcus, puzzled.

"Not just any key. It is the only one of its kind."

"It looks like a regular key to me."

"Ah, but therein lies the magic," replied Zyll. "With
this key, you will find within yourself more power than
you can now imagine. It will unlock your very destiny."

Placing the key in Marcus's hand, Zyll gestured toward
the hearth. "Try it once more."

The key felt heavy and cold. The tarnished iron was worn smooth in spots. Still Marcus sensed its power as he grasped it firmly in his fist. As he held the key at eye level, a peculiar tingling sensation spread through his fingers and wrist.

"Ignite!" Marcus commanded. At first, only the faintest crackle could be heard. Next, a small speck of orange glowed from the back of the hearth. Marcus leaned forward and blew air through his lips to fan an ember. On his first breath the glow intensified, then began to spread with the second. On the third breath, there was a loud pop as the ember leapt from the hearth, setting the hem of Zyll's robe on fire.

Marcus gasped in horror at his mistake. Without a moment's hesitation, he grabbed the kettle of soup and threw its contents at his master. The fire was put out, and from the sour expression on Zyll's face, so was he.

Marcus's shoulders drooped in dismay. "I'm sorry," he said.

Zyll shook off the bits of carrot and onion that clung to his robe. "No harm done, though I could have doused the flame myself and still had soup for my supper." Reaching for his walking stick, he announced, "It is time to go."

Zyll opened the cottage door and stepped outside. Marcus followed, the satchel hanging from his shoulder as limp as a large leather blossom wilting in the afternoon sun.

Two

The village of Quendel buzzed with an unusual amount of energy this morning. Zyll led the way with his walking staff while Marcus followed behind, doing his best to avoid stepping on the enchanter's robe, which slithered along the ground behind him like a snake.

Zyll's staff—carved from a branch of a Willenberry tree—was half the height of a full-grown man. Its top was carved into the shape of an eagle's head. From there the staff twisted its way toward the ground, where it tapered to a fine point. Zyll referred to this walking staff as "Xerxes" and often spoke to it as if it were a living being. Of course, the staff never spoke back. It just gazed forward with lifeless eyes.

9

Quendel was not unlike all the other villages east of the Jeweled Mountains, with its clusters of humble cottages and shops connected by narrow cobbled roads. Marcus closed his eyes a moment, allowing the sounds and smells of the place to calm his nerves. He never tired of the fragrance of warm bread drifting out of the baker's door, or the nutty scent of freshly ground wheat from the grain mill. Also, the constant clamor of wagons bumping along the roads and the bleating and braying of the animals that pulled them were a welcome contrast to the pervasive silence of Zyll's isolated dwelling.

As Marcus and Zyll made their way toward the stone water fountain at the center of town, Marcus overheard fragments of conversations between some of the villagers. "What were they thinking?" said one man, measuring out grain into another man's sack. A woman with a wailing child in her arms clucked to her neighbor, "He doesn't stand a chance." Other villagers stared at Marcus, their voices lowering to whispers as he passed by. The hot feeling in the pit of Marcus's stomach told him they were talking about him, and knowing that made him all the more anxious.

A wooden platform had been erected in front of the fountain. Master Zyll instructed Marcus to step up on it. As he did so, Marcus scanned the crowd. The streets and area surrounding the fountain were packed with so many people that he could not see the stones beneath their feet. Children sat on their fathers' shoulders or in wooden handcarts. Women, their skin browned from laboring alongside their husbands in the fields, strained on tiptoe to see past the men. As the center of so much attention, Marcus felt like a horse on the auction block. He glanced at the other five boys who stood with him. He had known them all since childhood, though as an orphan and Zyll's apprentice, his time spent with his peers had been limited to weapons training and occasional field games.

The boy immediately to Marcus's left was Jerrid Zwelger, the governor's pompous nephew, who sported a glossy new satchel and his usual smug expression. Jerrid stood in what Marcus thought to be a comical pose, hands on his hips and chin jutting out proudly. It was as though he thought the entire village had come only for him.

Beside Jerrid stood gangly, freckle-faced Zody Smythe, Jerrid's closest friend and disciple. Short for his age and on the scrawny side, Zody appeared as ill at ease on the platform as Jerrid was confident. He stood behind the other boys, preferring not to be noticed at all.

Next in the row was Clovis Dungham. Clovis, who was on the plump side, was fidgeting nervously with his pack, trying to loosen the strap across his shoulder. When the strap finally slipped through its buckle, Clovis beamed with satisfaction—until he realized that the strap was now too loose.

Tristan Tether came next. His ancestors had long ago emigrated from the mainland, and his russet complexion set him apart from the lighter-skinned islanders, though no one in Quendel seemed to notice or care. With his hand raised to his brow, he searched the crowd. Someone

waved frantically from the mass of onlookers. Marcus
thought it was impossible to tell who was waving, but
Tristan waved back just the same. A few moments later,
one of the local girls pushed her way through the throng
toward the platform. As she ran forward, Tristan dropped
to his knees. The girl threw her arms around his neck and
kissed him, all while tying a bright yellow scarf around his
neck. Then just as quickly, the girl blended back into the
crowd, crying audibly.

Marcus had to lean far forward to see who was at the
end of the row of boys. Standing with his shoulders
squared and his back erect, golden hair combed neatly
behind his ears, was Kelvin Archer.

Kelvin was the oldest and tallest of the group, his
birthday falling just one week shy of last year's ceremony.
He was therefore the most respected and admired boy in
his age group. However, if he derived any pleasure from
his status, he never showed it. He was a quiet boy and
sought no one's company but his own.

Marcus felt rather plain compared to Kelvin. His own
hair was straw-colored, his eyes a dull hazel. He was several inches shorter than Kelvin and considered himself
much too thin.

A horn sounded. Squire Slermin, Governor of Quendel,
stood before the crowd and raised his hands for silence.
"Today marks an epic moment in Quendelian history!" he
began. "These boys who stand before you shall embark on
a grand quest. If all goes well, they shall return to us no
longer boys, but men!"

The crowd burst into roaring applause. Another horn sounded, and the crowd grew silent. A knot formed in Marcus's throat. His mouth was dry as flint, and the perspiration ran down his face in tiny rivulets.

The squire spoke now in a hushed tone. The anticipation in the air was so heavy that Marcus felt it pressing against him. "My good people, it is time for that momentous occasion when the wisest and oldest of our kind pronounces the commencement of this year's *Bleôth Camrū*. I give you now: Master Zyll."

As the squire stepped down from the platform, the water in the fountain began to swirl in wide circles, which soon reached up toward the sky until a column of water churned in the air before them. All of a sudden the column burst like a giant bubble, sending a fine spray across the platform. The boys and those nearest to the fountain covered their faces to avoid the shower, while the rest of the crowd let out a collective gasp of admiration. When they returned their gaze to the platform, they found Zyll standing in the settling mist.

"On this day of the equinox, this moment of balance and equality, I summon the gods to grant divine protection upon you boys as you begin your journey into manhood. May you be wise, courageous, and cautious in your travels, and may you return to us both unharmed and victorious. Though the journey ahead will be difficult, you must remain undaunted, focused on the task. Those who succeed in this quest will bring the greatest of honors upon Quendel and upon themselves."

Those who succeed. The words repeated themselves in Marcus's mind, and he felt the weight of this responsibility descend heavily upon his young shoulders. It was a burden he felt driven to carry.

"And now, my sons," continued Zyll, sweeping his staff over the heads of the six boys, "it is time to reveal the nature of your journey. Your quest is . . ."

Here Zyll's voice paused, allowing his words to settle on the waiting crowd. Marcus counted the seconds that passed in unbearable silence. The other boys shifted anxiously beside him.

"Your quest is to find the Rock of Ivanore and bring it back to Quendel."

The boys glanced at each other, puzzled. Jerrid Zwelger cleared his throat and stepped forward.

"Master Zyll," he said, "we heard rumors that we'd be hunting warboars in the Black Forest."

Zyll struck Xerxes roughly against the platform. "You may hunt warboars if you wish, but it is the Rock of Ivanore you are required to pursue! Now, be off with you!"

Zyll pointed Xerxes in the direction of the forest, but not a boy moved from his spot. They remained as bewildered as before. Finally, it was Marcus who spoke up. "But Master," he said in almost a whisper, "what *is* the Rock of Ivanore? And where will we find it?"

The old man's lips trembled as he ground his teeth. Once again he pointed the end of his staff to the forest, jabbing it in the air like the point of a sword. "You will never find the Rock of Ivanore by standing here wiping your noses on your mothers' aprons! Go on, all of you! Go on before I pronounce you all failures and assign you to a lifetime of weeding the marshes!"

The boys all hurried off the platform and disappeared one by one through the nearby trees with the clanking of weapons and tin plates echoing behind them. Before Marcus could follow, he felt the weight of a hand on his shoulder.

"I do not wish for you to travel alone on this journey," said Zyll, his usual subdued mood returned. He grasped his staff around its middle with his right hand and held it so that his face met the eagle's, nose to beak. The eagle's eyes stared blankly forward. "So, Xerxes, it seems the day has come that we must part. I expect you will be as worthy a companion to this boy as you have been to me. What's that now?" Then Zyll added with a hearty laugh, "Oh, I can manage with an old hickory branch to lean upon."

Zyll held out the staff to Marcus. "Take him," he said, "before I change my mind and give *you* the hickory branch instead."

Marcus hesitated. He did not wish to take his master's staff, not only because Zyll was in such great need of it, but also because it had long been the butt of many jokes among his peers. And now, if he were to be seen with it, surely their jokes would be directed at him.

Marcus was about to decline the gift when he made the mistake of looking at his master's eyes. Never before had Marcus seen the expression they now wore. All at once it conveyed to Marcus Zyll's deep love for Xerxes—

and for him. So he said nothing, taking the staff and nodding his thanks. Zyll stepped down from the platform and walked briskly away. He stopped abruptly and turned.

"What is it, boy?" Zyll shouted, waving his hand as if shooing away a lazy rooster. "Must I light a fire underfoot to get you to move?"

Marcus smiled at his master's performance, for he knew that Zyll was not really angry with him.

"Mind you care for Xerxes as your own," Zyll advised as though he were delegating to Marcus the care of a young child. "Treat him well, and you'll find he's just full of surprises!" he added with a chuckle. "And bring him back to me in one piece, if you please!"

Marcus waved Xerxes above his head in a final goodbye. He swung his satchel over his shoulder and checked his pocket to see that the key Zyll had given him was still in its place. Then he hurried forward, eager for whatever adventures awaited.

Three

Far away from the village of Quendel, on the shore of Illian Bay, the half-breed pulled his small but sturdy vessel from the sea. He removed the scroll from beneath his cloak and unrolled it onto the dry sand, weighing down its corners with stones. He was certain he had landed in the correct cove and that a path through the forest waited nearby. He must only find it—a task he expected would not prove difficult, for he had Agoran blood flowing through his veins. His eyes, gray as ash, were more catlike than human in both appearance and ability. Though only half Agoran, still he could discern greater detail than his human cousins, a talent that gave him confidence that he could succeed where few humans had before him.

The Isle of Imaness was a formidable fortress, encircled by high, menacing cliffs and merciless tides. Many ships had met an unfortunate fate by them. Only two safe harbors existed along its shores. The first was a treacherous inlet on the northwestern border of the province of Dokur. The other lay at the southernmost tip of the island—the gently sloping sands of Illian Bay.

Guarded by jagged rocks that stood like armed sentinels along the shore, the northwestern coast was doubly secure due to the vigilant Eye of Dokur, a lofty tower overlooking the bay. No ship approached Dokur unseen, and the half-breed Agoran had his reasons for concealing his arrival.

The only other choice was to approach Imaness through Illian Bay, safeguarded only by an ancient forest whose vegetation wound so tightly together that traveling through it was all but impossible. The only hope in navigating through the tangled Black Forest lay in the legendary map drawn by the island's ancient inhabitants.

The Agoran paced the beach, peering at every vine and leaf. He prodded branches and briars with the tip of his sword, but the centuries-old undergrowth was so dense that it seemed as though nothing could penetrate it. He studied the scroll again, tracing its lines with his finger and measuring each twist and turn of ink. Again and again, he walked the distance from one end of the beach to the other, each time comparing more closely the image on the page to the forest's perimeter.

He had just finished his fourth tour of the beach when something small, nearly indistinguishable, caught his

attention. A small green thread as thin as spider's silk
dangled from a single leaf. A sense of relief washed over
him, for someone with eyesight less keen than his would
never have spotted it at all. The patch of vegetation blended so perfectly with its surroundings that it was nearly
impossible to detect its true material: delicate green cloth
painted by the finest of artisans.

The Agoran pulled away the false cover, revealing a
narrow but definite trail. He rolled up the parchment and
tucked it beneath his cloak. As he did so, his hand brushed
against the leather pouch hanging at his waist. The first
object in the fist-sized pouch had been with him for many
years and had brought him, he believed, good fortune. It
was a rare treasure, and he had killed and nearly been
killed for it. The second item in the pouch was obtained
more recently but was equally valuable to its new owner.

The Agoran wrapped his palm around the pouch to
reassure himself. It felt warm and soft in his hand. He
rubbed his thumb along its seam and hoped it would
bring him good fortune one last time. Then, stepping
onto the trail and setting the shrubbery back in place
behind him, he ventured forward into the shadows of
the forest.

Four

Marcus spent the good part of the day walking in what he hoped was a straight course west along the northern edge of the forest. If he continued on that same course, he expected to reach Vrystal Canyon, the only passage through the mountains, by nightfall.

Marcus stopped near a small brook and sat down. Just a few moments' rest is all I need, he thought to himself. His eyes grew heavy and had barely closed when the loud snap of a twig jerked them open.

"Who's there?" he called out.

A familiar voice called back. "It's just me!"

Clovis Dungham, the heavyset boy from the ceremony, ran clumsily forward. His pack, with its loose strap slung around his elbow, banged wildly against his thigh.

His breathing was heavy.

"I've been trying . . . to catch up to you . . . thought maybe . . . we could . . ." He paused, bent over, and gasped for breath.

"Are you all right?" asked Marcus, concerned that Clovis might faint.

Clovis nodded. "Couldn't catch my breath at first," he said. His round face was red and damp with perspiration. "Sometimes I have trouble breathing . . . when I exercise too much." He took a swig from his water skin. "I thought, maybe . . . if you're not opposed to it . . . I might keep you company . . . for a while at least."

Marcus considered telling him that he preferred to travel alone, but then he noticed the crossbow slung across the other boy's back. "Can you really use that thing?" he asked. "How good is your aim?"

Clovis sniffed. It seemed he was sniffling every few seconds. "Not half as well as my father. He can shoot a sparrow in flight. He lent me this," he added, reaching over his shoulder and patting the bow fondly, "but made me promise to return it in good condition."

The two of them continued walking together, and Marcus found he was glad for the company. "Have you seen any of the others?" he asked after a while.

"Not since we left home," replied Clovis. "But before we divided up, I heard Jerrid say he's going to try to cut through the forest."

Marcus had heard stories of the Black Forest and the terrifying creatures that lived among the entangled trunks and limbs. Anyone who was presumptuous enough to think he could get through it and live was either naïve or arrogant—and Jerrid Zwelger was both.

"Of course *he'd* try a shortcut," said Marcus. "He wants the Rock of Ivanore for himself."

"Do you really think so?"

"He's been boasting for weeks about how he's going to finish the quest before the rest of us—not content to share the glory, I suppose."

"Well, I for one hope we find the Rock of Ivanore quickly," said Clovis. "I've never been away from home before."

"But how can any of us find it if we don't even know what it is?" Marcus felt annoyed that Zyll had not at least given him a clue as to the rock's location.

"I think it's something magical," Clovis suggested.

"What makes you say that?"

"I overheard my parents talking with the Archers about it once, though I only heard snippets. Supposed to be powerful enough to build and destroy entire kingdoms."

Marcus laughed. "Sounds like a fable to me."

"Maybe, but . . . oh no!" Clovis stopped abruptly and pinched his nose.

"What's wrong?" Marcus dropped his satchel to the ground and hurried to Clovis's side. A thin, red line trickled down Clovis's upper lip.

"It's nothing," he whined in a muffled, nasal voice. "Just a bloody nose. I get them sometimes. Quite often, actually. I'm fine. Really."

"Are you sure?" Marcus glanced up through the trees. Daylight would be fading soon, and they had not traveled half the distance he had hoped to.

"I'll be fine in a few minutes," said Clovis, "half an hour at most."

Marcus sat down on a boulder jutting out from the soft earth and wished he had brought one of Zyll's books along for the journey. "It'll be dusk by then," he said. "We might as well camp here."

"I don't mind going on," said Clovis. "We could reach Vrystal Canyon in two or three hours."

"The sun's going down," replied Marcus. He was beginning to regret letting Clovis come along. Clovis released his nose, but the blood still flowed freely. He pinched it again.

"Nearly clotted," he said apologetically. "In five minutes, I'll be ready to go—"

"I told you, we're making camp!" snapped Marcus. The moment he did so, he regretted the outburst. He looked away from the stunned expression on Clovis's face, afraid his own shame was apparent.

"I'm sorry," he said. "I didn't mean to lose my temper. It's just that—" He felt his cheeks grow warm. "I don't like the dark."

He was certain that Clovis would burst into laughter. Marcus, nearly a man and afraid of the dark. But there was no laughter.

"Oh," said Clovis, as though the news were as trivial as a fruit fly. "We'll need wood for the fire then. Shall I go?"

Marcus smiled at his companion, whose nostrils were still clamped in the vise-like grip of his fingers. "I'll go," he said and set off to gather wood in the forest.

When he returned, he found Clovis devouring a plump slice of roasted quail, his nosebleed all but forgotten. "Mother packed it for me," Clovis said through greasy lips. Marcus eyed the meat hungrily and reached into his satchel. Just as he had feared, his bread had turned to crumbs. He licked up a handful of the bland fragments of his dinner.

"I'll start the fire," he said, clearing a spot of earth and arranging the kindling he had gathered. He reached in his pocket for his key. It was a simple key, just a finger-length rod of iron with a plain oval loop on one end and a notched extrusion at the other. Still, it would not be wise to judge any charm solely on its appearance.

He gripped the key in his left hand and waved his other over the kindling. "Ignite!" he commanded. Not a flicker appeared. He waved his hand again and repeated the order, but the wood remained stubborn.

"I've got flint and wool," offered Clovis, but Marcus ignored him.

"Ignite, you stupid shrub, ignite!" When the fourth attempt was equally unsuccessful, Marcus sheepishly put away the key for Clovis's flint and wool. The fire soon engulfed the tinder and Marcus added to it three larger logs. He warmed his hands against the flames. He then removed his cape and spread it out on the ground, resting on it with his back to the fire. Beside him, Clovis did the same and was soon fast asleep.

Marcus searched the darkening night with wide eyes, but except for the small circle of light cast by the fire, the forest was as black as coal. He could see nothing but the faint silhouette of the nearest trees; the thought of what might lie beyond them made him apprehensive. To calm himself, he turned his thoughts to the quest and to tomorrow's journey. He knew of a library in Noam, a town on the other side of the mountains, and thought that might be a good place to inquire about the Rock of Ivanore.

The sound of Clovis snoring convinced him he had better rest as well. He laid down his head on his satchel and closed his eyes. Meanwhile, from the safety of a low-hanging tree branch, a pair of eyes watched him as he slept, their pupils narrowed into fine slits as they studied him.

Five

On the opposite side of the Isle of Imaness, the sleepy city of Dokur lay atop a sprawling plateau, as content in its security as a napping lion. The claw-like rock formations encircling the harbor were as menacing as the most lethal of weapons. The great tower looked out over the rocky shores of Imaness like an ever-present sentry, and no enemy ever dared approach the island under its ominous gaze. To do so would be to play into the hands of fate toward a certain defeat by means of the royal navy.

No one escaped the Eye of Dokur.

Perched on the hill just behind the tower, the Fortress appeared from a distance to be no more than a child's toy planted on some lonely dune. But those who lived in the settlement beneath knew the truth about its menacing power and shuddered to think of it. They preferred to go about their business as discreetly as possible, doing nothing to single themselves out from the mass or to attract the attention of His Lordship of Dokur.

Only one dared to wander from the city and stand upon the cliffs to watch the sea. Every day at twilight, the young woman lay down her bundle of kindling to stare at the vast blue horizon. Almost fifteen years had passed since she had begun this ritual—nearly a lifetime of breaking away from the ebb and flow of daily routine to which everyone else was so fettered. But no one seemed to care or even notice. Not even the Eye of Dokur wasted energy on the dark-haired woman with the distant look in her eyes, the one known only as Mouse.

She had first come to Dokur when she was five years old. A wayward child, she spent her days in the streets scrounging for food; her nights were spent on the cliffs. When people asked her about her home and her parents, she said nothing, choosing instead to meet their questions with a defiant, tight-lipped stare. At some point she began working to earn her keep. A full belly and a warm bed were temptations no child could resist. She worked long hours, often to the point of exhaustion, but no matter where she was or what she was doing, at dusk she always came back to the cliffs.

Mouse sat on her boulder with her knees to her chest and counted the stars as they appeared one by one overhead. The sun had long since descended beneath the distant sea, and her stomach told her she had better get back to the tavern soon or there would be hell to pay. But she chose instead to wait a while longer, braving the owner's inevitable wrath.

Was it the anxious churning in her chest that anchored her there tonight, or was it the ever-increasing hopelessness she felt? She thought if she could somehow hold on one moment longer, she just might catch a glimpse of that fading hope on the horizon. Yet it was not to be. With a slow, disheartened sigh, she hefted her bundle to her shoulder and made her way down the path to town.

Six

arcus fell into a deep and comforting sleep. In his dreams he smelled the scent of fresh leather, felt the stiff edges of a fine strap between his fingers. He imagined that inside his new satchel he carried the most delicious fare: hot corn fritters bathed in sweet Willenberry sauce, dried pears, and squares of rich fudge. As he prepared to devour this feast, a loud screech shattered his vision.

Marcus sat up abruptly. He rubbed his eyes, still cloudy from sleep, and searched the darkness for the source of the sound, but all was now quiet. Only a cricket's lullaby and Clovis Dungham's rhythmic breathing reached his ears.

He stabbed at the remains of the fire with a stick. The orange coals spit hot sparks back at him. He watched the

ever-changing flames while absentmindedly fingering the
key his master had given him. It felt smooth and cold—
and strangely comforting.

With heavy eyes, Marcus was about to lie back down
when the screech tore through the night once more. The
high-pitched shriek sounded almost human, as if someone
had cried out in pain—or fear.

The screech sounded a third time. "Watch out!" it
screamed.

Marcus leapt to his feet and spun around. There,
above the glow of the dying embers, were two yellow eyes.
At first it appeared as if the two glassy spheres hovered in
the darkness, but as they began to sway back and forth and
came forward into the light, Marcus saw that the eyes
belonged to the biggest snake he had ever seen.

The snake slid through the glowing embers, its thick
body seemingly endless as it curled itself into an enormous
coil directly in front of Marcus. Its massive forked tongue
flicked at the air as if tasting it. Then, to Marcus's surprise,
the serpent spoke. "The foresssst issss no place for man," it
said. Its voice was a deep, drawn-out whisper, not like the
shriek Marcus heard before. "Perhapssss man isss losssst?"

Marcus tried to hold himself steady despite the fact
that his entire body trembled with fear. "I'm not lost," he
said. "I'm only passing through this part of the forest."

"Passssing through?" The snake's pupils dilated and
then narrowed to slits again. "Alone?"

Marcus glanced at Clovis sleeping on the ground. Had
the serpent not noticed him?

His stomach felt queasy. He was afraid his knees would buckle at any moment, but he managed to remain standing. The snake met his gaze and held it for a long while before rearing its head high in the air. Its gaze bore down on Marcus's quivering frame.

The snake responded to his own question. "Yessss, alone. On a long journey. Sssooooo no one sssshould missss you for sssome time." The snake opened its jaws so wide that Marcus could have stepped inside without hitting his head. Though Marcus was inclined to run, the absolute terror of the moment glued his feet to the ground.

The snake lunged forward, and as it did so, Marcus instinctively threw his hands over his face. To his surprise, Zyll's key grew hot in his hand, so hot it burned him, and he nearly dropped it from the pain. At the same moment, the embers from the fire flared up, and a pillar of flame spiraled upward, scorching the serpent's tender underbelly. The snake shrank back in pain but quickly prepared for another attack.

Suddenly, from out of the darkness a figure leapt at the snake, the hilt of a dagger flashing in the fire's glow. There was a struggle, a low, deep moan—and then silence.

When Marcus opened his eyes he found the snake half-coiled and dead at his feet. A trail of blood ran out of its mouth, soaking the earth.

Marcus peered through the darkness. "Wh-who are you?" The figure stepped forward, firelight casting dancing shadows upon his golden hair and fine features.

"Kelvin Archer!" cried Marcus. All at once he felt relieved—and embarrassed.

"I heard you scream," said Kelvin. He wiped his dagger clean with a handful of leaves and nodded toward Clovis, still sleeping soundly.

"Remind me not to call on him for help if ever the need arises," he said, sliding the dagger into a leather scabbard strapped about his waist. Clovis mumbled something incoherent and rolled over onto his side. Oblivious, he continued to snore long into the night.

Seven

The high branches of the forest trees formed a tight green canopy overhead. So entwined were they that only the most persistent rays of sunlight had broken through, casting thin, yellow beams of light through layered shadows. But now that day had turned to night, the forest seemed an eternal abyss of darkness.

The Agoran half-breed held his cloak tightly around him to prevent it from getting caught in the thorny underbrush. Using his sword, he continued to hack his way through the forest one step at a time. Though he had traveled all day, his progress was much slower than he had hoped. He knew the trail led directly to the mouth of Vrystal Canyon, the only known passage between the west and east sides of the island. However, the path proved a greater obstacle than he had anticipated. Even with his keen eyesight, the Agoran struggled to follow the trail, which had long since been shrouded by vines. The trees seemed to close in on him, suffocating him, until every part of his being screamed for him to turn back in defeat.

If I stay on this course, he thought to himself, I will never reach Dokur in time.

Had he the benefit of companions, each with a blade and a pair of strong arms, he could have cleared the trail in a matter of hours. Alone it would take days—and time was a luxury he did not have. Taking a moment to review the map on the scroll, the Agoran revised his plan. By shifting his path slightly west, he calculated that the distance through the Black Forest would be one mile instead of five. He would simply have to find some other way to reach the canyon.

His determination renewed, he struck at the thick, gnarled branches with his blade. Despite his slow progress, he expected to reach the outskirts of the surrounding forest by midnight.

The full moon was high overhead when the Agoran finally broke through the last barricade of branches. The silvery glow was a welcome sight, but not as welcome as the sheer cliff that rose directly above him. Since the forest grew right up to the foot of the cliff, reaching the canyon on level ground would be impractical. He would have to go over the mountains.

The Agoran sheathed his sword and made certain that the scroll, his drinking skin, and the prized leather pouch were all fastened securely. While the sheer granite face might prove an impossible obstacle to most men, for the Agoran—whose catlike claws were as sharp and sturdy as iron nails—it was a welcome challenge.

The muscles in his arms and chest bulged as he began his ascent. The chill in the air cooled his skin and invigorated his climbing. He recalled the races he had won as a child, climbing rocks and trees in record time. What he lacked in agility, he more than compensated for with his strength. His human bone structure supported a denser musculature than those of his full-blooded Agoran peers, and he never failed to take advantage of it. Now, as he rose high above the forest, it seemed as though he could simply reach out his hand and grasp the stars. As he gazed out over the island, he considered for a moment the peace solitude had brought. He could still go back, he thought briefly, but instead shook off the temptation and increased his rate of ascent. He had lived in seclusion long enough. He had to reach Dokur soon—no matter what the cost.

Eight

The sounds of the nighttime forest were enough to cause even the bravest of hearts to quicken in fear, but Kelvin slept sprawled out on the ground, seemingly unafraid of anything real or imaginary. Marcus, on the other hand, sat with his back against a tall boulder, his eyes wide, scanning the darkness. He would not allow himself to be taken by surprise again.

Midnight had come and gone when Marcus finally convinced himself that it was safe to close his eyes and sleep. Just as his mind began to drift, he heard the voice again, though it was not a screech like before, but high-pitched nonetheless.

"Lie down and sleep, you stupid boy!"

Marcus was on his feet in an instant, scanning the forest, his lungs gasping for air, his heart racing. "Who said that?" he hissed.

"What do you mean 'who said that'?" the voice retorted.

It sounded quite near, but Marcus saw only rocks and trees and endless darkness.

"Where are you?" Marcus called out.

The voice called back. "Here!"

"Where? I don't see anything!"

"That is because you are as blind as you are stupid, boy! I am here against the rock!"

Marcus looked toward the boulder, against which only a moment earlier he had been resting. Leaning against it was Zyll's walking stick.

Marcus approached cautiously. Kneeling beside the boulder, he examined the wooden eagle head. Nothing seemed different than before. The stiff, wooden face stared blankly forward like it always had. Marcus rubbed his eyes, blaming exhaustion for playing tricks on his mind. Then suddenly there was movement. A flicker of eyelids, a ruffling of dull, brown feathers, and a beak opening.

"Xerxes?" Marcus gaped at the bird.

"The boy's a genius after all," said Xerxes sarcastically.

"But this is impossible—"

The bird squawked loudly. "Impossible for whom? What is so impossible about an enchanted walking stick?"

"It was *you* who screamed?" asked Marcus, recalling the screeching that had led Kelvin to his rescue.

Xerxes' image moved as if it were a living bird. His

eyes opened and shut, as did his beak when he spoke. If it weren't for his plain, brown surface so obviously carved from wood, Marcus might have sworn it was a real bird before him instead of a walking stick.

"You saved my life," said Marcus. "If you hadn't screamed out when you did, that snake might have swallowed me in my sleep."

Xerxes rolled his eyes and clicked his beak. "You could have saved your own life if you had only used that brain of yours. Take off my head."

"What?"

Xerxes repeated his command. "Take . . . off . . . my . . . head! But replace it quickly, as I cannot speak when separated from my staff."

Marcus obediently grasped Xerxes' head in his hands, giving it a firm twist. It pulled away from the rest of the wood, revealing a long, slender steel blade. Marcus inspected the weapon with awe and then sheathed the sword. "Zyll said you were full of surprises," he said. "Thank you for helping me."

"Master Zyll made me swear to get you back alive," said Xerxes. "So how could I sit idly by and watch you get swallowed whole by a serpent? If I had done that, this stone might very well have been my only companion for a long time to come. Not that it isn't a good conversationalist, mind you, only . . ." Xerxes' voice dropped to a whisper, and Marcus leaned forward to hear him. "It's just that the stone's a bit of a gossip, that's all, and I simply detest gossips, don't you?"

Marcus thought of Zyll and the teasing the enchanter had endured as a result of this thing. He wondered why his master would burden him with such a disagreeable companion. Still, he *had* asked Zyll for a weapon.

"So, are you to be my guide?" asked Marcus.

The bird rolled its eyes again. "Heavens, no! I'm no guide. You have the key for that job."

"The key? Zyll told me it would lead me to my destiny, but how is that possible when I can't even get it to work?"

"That is no ordinary key," explained Xerxes. "It was forged in the depths of Voltana from the four elements: earth, air, water, and fire. Use it well, and you will become a mighty enchanter indeed."

Marcus still held the key in his hand, and he now examined it more closely. "When the snake attacked me, the key got hot in my hand."

"Yes," replied Xerxes, "and the fire surged at your command!"

"But I gave no command."

"You did not speak it, but in your heart you called for the key's protection, and it heeded you. Yet beware. The power of that key may be more than a boy like you can wield."

"What do you mean?" pressed Marcus. "I can't even get it to obey my simplest request."

"You will with time," Xerxes explained. "I am to train you. In the morning, rise early before the others awake. We will begin tomorrow. Now," added Xerxes, "you have kept me awake long enough! I must get some sleep!"

Xerxes gave one brief, screeching yawn, and then closed his beady eyes.

Marcus lay down on the earth beside him, his mind churning with everything Xerxes had told him. He gazed up at the stars and, after a while, started to count them. He insisted to himself that he wasn't in the least bit tired, but he soon lost count and drifted off to sleep.

Nine

t's just a dream.

Marcus repeated those words over and over in his mind, but the night suffocated him like a damp, dark shroud from which he could not escape. He struggled for breath. Rolling to his side, he dug his fingers into the loose soil, desperate to escape the unseen power that bound him. Then suddenly a light appeared, just as he had dreamed a hundred times before. In the light he saw the figure of—what was it?—an angel?

The image was difficult to make out in the bright light, and Marcus raised his hand to shield his eyes. The angel came to him, reached out for him, but as Marcus stretched out his hands toward it, something pulled him back.

Something black and sinister was overpowering him. He struggled to resist it. He called to the angel to help him, but the light receded until he was left again in darkness.

Marcus jerked open his eyes. The darkness that greeted him caused momentary alarm, but the sound of Xerxes' voice reassured him that the dream was over.

"Just how much sleep does an orphan boy need?" Xerxes was asking.

Marcus rubbed his eyes and stretched, his heart still pounding. Clovis and Kelvin slept beside him, their positions unchanged from hours earlier.

"Let's get on with this, shall we?" said Xerxes. "We'll find a spot through those trees."

Marcus hesitated. He could not even see the outline of the trees to which Xerxes referred. "It's too dark," he said, lifting Xerxes in his hand and holding him close. "I can't see where I'm going."

"A good first lesson, then." Xerxes craned back his neck and twisted his head from side to side. "I'm a bit stiff from that damp night air," he said. "Now, take out the key."

Marcus obeyed.

"What do you want the key to do?" Xerxes asked.

"I don't know," said Marcus, shrugging his shoulders. "I want light."

"Don't tell *me*!" scolded Xerxes. "Tell the wretched key!"

Marcus held up the key between his thumb and forefinger. Its shape was hard to distinguish in the darkness, but as he formed the word *light* upon his lips, the key began to glow just enough to illuminate a shallow path through the trees.

Once he and Xerxes were a safe distance from the camp, Marcus let out a gleeful shout. "I did it!" he said, hardly containing his excitement. "The key obeyed me!"

"I wouldn't feel so proud if I were you," replied Xerxes. "Light is the simplest of effects. Even a babe could manage it."

Marcus tried not to feel deflated by Xerxes' comments, but it was hard not to. He pushed his wounded pride aside and focused on Xerxes' next instructions.

"Zyll explained the nature of magic, of manipulating the elements, did he not? Now you must learn the art of transmutation."

"Transforming one element into another," said Marcus, recalling a recent lesson in alchemy.

"Yes," continued Xerxes, "but it's not what you might think. Many a foolish man has wasted his life trying to turn rocks into gold. They've died in poverty, every single one of them—and they deserved it."

"So what is transmutation, then?"

"Simply changing the state or nature of an object by manipulating the elements around or within it. For instance, should you come across a river that needs crossing, withdraw its heat and turn it to ice. Need to dig a hole? Move the soil. Repair a broken wall? Mend the iron and granite within the crack."

Marcus thought of the satchel that hung from his shoulder. "I would like to mend this thing," he said.

"Leather is organic; it has been taken from a living thing, as has wood, flesh, and foliage," explained Xerxes. "You can manipulate energy or inorganic materials to affect it, but to transform an organic object itself is nearly impossible. Not even the great Zyll will do it."

"Why is it impossible?"

Xerxes clicked his beak impatiently. "Enough questions. Time for your lesson."

Marcus leaned Xerxes against the nearest tree. He wanted to know more about the limits of his magic, but he dared not irritate his new teacher.

"You will liquefy that stone over there," directed Xerxes. "Take out your key. Harvest your energy and bring it into focus."

The stone was unimpressive, just a round rock about the size of a bread loaf. Marcus held out the key and closed his eyes. He tried to form an image of the stone in his mind, tried to see it softening and melting upon his command. He could not, however, locate the energy he needed for such a feat—at least not in the dark.

"I can't do it," he said, shaking his head, annoyed with himself. "There's no energy here."

"There is always energy," replied Xerxes. "As long as your heart is beating and your lungs take in air, there is energy."

"Maybe that's true, but I can't even light a fire."

"That will come in time," said Xerxes, though the exasperated tone in his voice was far from comforting. "Try it again, but first you will need to douse the key's glow so that it can work the other spell."

Marcus let the key dim. He turned his thoughts outward. Once again Marcus imagined the stone transforming into a pool of liquid granite. He reached deep inside himself, drawing on his own life force for the energy he needed to perform the task. The key's temperature rose slightly in his hand. Marcus grinned in spite of himself, for he sensed the stone's core absorbing heat.

Without warning, the stone exploded. The loud blast resounded off every tree and boulder. Bits of rock and soil shot out in all directions and rained down around Marcus. When the dust began to settle, Marcus brushed fragments of his failure from his hair, face, and shoulders. He was just wiping Xerxes free of it when Kelvin burst through the trees gasping for breath. Marcus was relieved that Kelvin had had the sense to bring a lighted stick with him.

"What was that?" Kelvin asked, his eyes scanning the area for signs of danger. "It sounded like an explosion—or thunder."

Marcus shrugged dumbly, too shocked to speak.

"A storm must be gathering in the mountains," continued Kelvin, though his expression was one of uncertainty. "We should try to reach Noam before it rains." Kelvin turned and headed back toward the camp, kicking aside several small pebbles as he went.

"Thunder?" asked Xerxes once Kelvin was out of earshot. "Why didn't you answer him?"

"I panicked," replied Marcus. "What should I have said?"

"There is no need to hide your magic from him," Xerxes explained. "He knows you are Zyll's apprentice."

Marcus placed the key back in his pocket and started for camp. He felt weary and out of breath. "I'm sorry about the stone," he said, shaking off the feeling. "I'll do a better job of transmutation tomorrow."

Xerxes fluffed his wooden feathers and shook his head. "Perhaps, for the time being, you should concentrate on something less complicated," he said, "like staying out of danger for at least one day!"

Ten

arcus, Clovis, and Kelvin reached the mouth to Vrystal Canyon a few hours after sunrise. They set down their packs on a large moss-covered boulder and ate a bit of cheese for breakfast. When they were finished, Marcus stood at the canyon entrance and stared into the dark, narrow passageway flanked on either side by towering granite cliffs.

"Is there any other way around these cliffs?" Marcus asked, tucking the remainder of his food into his satchel.

Kelvin sharpened the edge of his dagger against a bare patch of stone. "Along the shoreline, maybe, but we would have to go through the forest."

Marcus surveyed the dense tangle of forest undergrowth. "Impossible," he concluded with a shake of his head.

As Kelvin sheathed his dagger and bent to adjust the scabbard at his waist, Marcus glimpsed what appeared to be some sort of pendant tucked just inside Kelvin's shirt. When Kelvin noticed his gaze, he quickly pulled up his collar around it.

"This is the only route," said Kelvin. "So if we want to reach Noam today, we'd better get going." He hoisted his pack to his left shoulder and disappeared into the canyon. Marcus let his eyes wander upward to scan the heights of the jagged skyline gaping open like a set of hungry jaws. The sight made him shiver.

He turned to Clovis, who was nursing another bloody nose. "Ready to go?"

Clovis shook his head. "I'll be here a while, I'm afraid," he said apologetically. "Why don't you go on ahead? I'll catch up later."

Marcus felt almost guilty for accepting the offer. He was anxious to reach Noam before nightfall. And Clovis would soon follow, he reasoned. After a quick good-bye, he hurried to catch up to Kelvin.

Daylight seemed to vanish the moment Marcus entered the canyon. A strange whooshing sound echoed off the canyon walls as a gust of wind shot through with a powerful force. Kelvin waited just inside. The boys covered their faces with their capes until the air grew still. Then they ventured forward slowly, steadily.

The walls were so close together Marcus could stretch out his arms and brush his fingers along both sides. They felt smooth, like the flat, round stones he had found in the old riverbed near his home, and they were covered in a thick layer of green algae.

"Zyll said this canyon is nearly as old as the island itself," Marcus said. "Legend has it the mountain shook one day and split wide open like a melon."

Kelvin shifted his pack from one shoulder to the other. "That's why it's legend. Look here." He scraped away some algae with his knife, revealing a patch of smooth rock. "A sudden rift would have left rough surfaces, like when a stone heats up in the fire. Pour water on it, and it'll crack and break open. The inner surface is always coarse and uneven."

"A ravine, then, made over time by moving water?" suggested Marcus.

"Maybe," replied Kelvin, though his face expressed doubt. "But we're walking on dry ground. And there's no evidence of any river, even a dry one." Kelvin replaced the dagger in its sheath. "The moisture seeps in through the cavern walls themselves. I believe we're passing through an underground reservoir. I just hope we make it through before sundown. Soon this place will be swarming with Grocs."

"Grocs?" Marcus shuddered. "They wouldn't bother us, would they?"

"As a rule, they hunt in the mountains. But last week a merchant from one of the coastal villages was attacked not far from here."

"Did he say what it was? What it looked like?" asked Marcus.

Kelvin shook his head. "The creature struck once, but it ran off before the merchant could get a good look at it. He showed me where it bit him, though," added Kelvin. He held up his clenched right hand. "It took a chunk out of his thigh as big as my fist."

The boys continued on, and though they were certain it was approaching midday, the air around them grew darker with each passing moment. Marcus's thoughts turned homeward. He tried to imagine what Zyll might be doing at that moment. Probably drawing water from the well, he realized, or preparing supper.

A little wave of melancholy passed through Marcus. "Do you think they'll miss you?" he asked Kelvin, more from a need to redirect his own thoughts than a need for an answer.

"Who?" Kelvin asked.

"Your mother and father. I saw you with them at the ceremony."

Kelvin's pace remained steady. "They're not my mother and father." His words were spoken as if stating a fact, no hint of emotion in his voice.

Marcus recalled that in all the years he had known Kelvin, the first time he had ever seen Mr. and Mrs. Archer was at the ceremony. Even at that momentous event, there was not the same affection between them as was visible between the other boys and their families. He had never considered the possibility that there might be another orphan beside himself in Quendel.

"If they aren't your parents, who are they?"

Before Kelvin could reply, a sharp and sudden cry stopped them in their tracks. Their hearts pounded so fast from the scare that Marcus thought they could almost hear one another's heartbeats.

"What was that?" he whispered. Kelvin held up a hand to silence him. Several yards ahead from where they stood, the walls curved so that their path was blocked from view. Neither boy dared to guess what might await them around the bend.

They did not have to wait long to find out.

Eleven

Kelvin drew his dagger. Marcus placed his hand on his walking stick, preparing to draw the sword. They advanced slowly until a figure stepped into view.

The being that stood before them now was not at all the fierce monster Marcus had expected. Rather, it was nothing more than a little boy with hair black as ebony and eyes the color of amber. His face was gentle, beseeching, his clothes rags. The boy stepped forward, his hands held out in front of him. Kelvin's dagger remained poised.

"Stay there!" Kelvin demanded.

The child shrank back in fear. Marcus, embarrassed by Kelvin's behavior, started toward the boy, but Kelvin held him back.

"Who are you?" said Kelvin roughly.

The boy bowed his head in an expression of servitude. "I am sorry," he said. His voice was soft and pleasing, like the gurgle of a gentle brook. "I did not wish to startle you. My name is Bryn. I have run out of food and water. I have no money, but I will work for it if you'll let me."

There was something unusual about the boy, something Marcus could not quite put his finger on. He told himself to be wary, that these parts were known to be swarming with undesirable creatures. But despite his anxiety, he also felt drawn to the child's pitiable countenance and wanted to help him.

"Kelvin," Marcus said, "we can spare a little food. He looks hungry." But Kelvin remained rigid as a stone, a look of utter contempt in his face.

"We don't have enough for three," Kelvin replied. "Move on, boy. Try your begging on someone else."

Bryn threw up his hands in a pleading gesture and dropped to his knees. "Do not send me away, I beg of you! Here . . ." and the boy scrambled froglike past them to where a heap of dried moss lay in the dirt. "It makes good kindling! Let me gather it along the way for your evening fire." He swept the entire bundle of moss into his arms and made as if ready to follow his new masters to the ends of the earth.

Marcus stepped between Bryn and Kelvin. "He's just a child," he reasoned. "How much would he eat, really? Why not let him come along? He might be useful to us."

Kelvin, grumbling, nodded his consent and sheathed his dagger. "Marcus, give him some bread if you like, but if there is any trouble, any trouble at all, or if he slows us down—"

Bryn bowed so low to the ground that his breath disturbed the dust at his feet. "Thank you, good master. I will be no trouble, I promise."

The three of them now continued their journey in the direction from which the boy had come. They had not gone far when another sound pierced the air. Xerxes' now-familiar shriek from the night before echoed against the canyon walls.

"Turn around!" Xerxes' voice seemed alarmed. "Turn around, you stupid boy!"

Marcus held back and waited until Kelvin and Bryn had walked a good distance ahead of him. The eagle's eyes had a wild look in them, and Marcus wondered what could cause such fear in the magic walking stick.

"Don't cry out like that," scolded Marcus in a whisper. "The others will hear you."

"No one can hear me but you. That is the curse of my existence," bemoaned Xerxes. "Only he who bears me can hear my words. It was Zyll's wish when he made me."

"But Kelvin heard your scream last night."

"And that is all he will ever hear. Mr. Archer is nothing but a brainless, arrogant fool. And whether you are brighter than he remains to be seen."

Marcus was becoming impatient. "Well, what did you want to tell me?"

"I saw something above," answered Xerxes. "'Twas only a shadow, but something is there, I tell you!"

"What do you mean? What shadow?"

"I do not know if it is the shadow of man or beast, but I have seen it several times now. It is stalking us from above."

Marcus turned his gaze upward to the top of the canyon, which was nearer now than it had been at its mouth. The cliff's edge was perhaps no more than twenty feet high, and the gap at the surface was so narrow Marcus guessed that a man could easily straddle it. The hairs on the back of his neck grew stiff, and a feeling of dread overcame him. Was it possible that someone—or something— was watching them from above?

Marcus let his question form words on his tongue. "Why would anyone follow us?" he asked. "We don't have anything worth stealing."

"Perhaps you are not the object of a *thief's* design," answered Xerxes. "Perhaps he is the hunter, and you . . ."

Here Xerxes' voice dropped to a whisper. "You are the prey!"

Twelve

As Xerxes returned to his inanimate form, Marcus became aware of the silence around him. Bryn and Kelvin had walked ahead and were no longer in his sight. Marcus sensed that something was wrong.

Marcus ran and within moments stumbled upon a gruesome sight. Kelvin lay unmoving on the ground. Bryn sat on his haunches beside him, his mouth stretched unnaturally wide like a python about to swallow its prey. His eyes glowed yellow. Upon seeing Marcus, the creature let out a deafening, animal-like howl.

"Leave him alone!" shouted Marcus. He rushed forward, swinging Xerxes like a club. The creature named Bryn leapt out of the way and slashed at Marcus's back with needle-like claws that had grown along its fingertips.

Marcus fell to his knees beside Kelvin. He could feel the blood trickling down his back. Despite his pain, though, Marcus acted quickly. Drawing the blade from the walking stick, he again lunged forward. Bryn snatched the blade between its teeth and yanked it out of Marcus's hands.

His heart pounding, Marcus tried desperately to plan his next course of action. He reached for Kelvin's dagger and brandished it in front of him.

"Stay back!" he threatened with a shaky voice. Bryn's boylike body had become distorted, its back humped and its limbs twisted. It laughed a deep, guttural laugh.

"I've no time for games," it said. "I'm hungry."

Marcus knew that he was no match for the creature. His only hope of escape lay with magic. As he wrapped his fingers around Zyll's key, he felt a warmth sweep through his hand and up his arm to his shoulder. He tried to recall the instructions his master had given him about concentrating heat into fire, but panic numbed his mind. When he felt certain that he could indeed cast the proper spell, he realized with dismay that they were in a rock canyon with no wood of any kind in sight, and the moss Bryn had carried was now scattered about everywhere.

The creature advanced toward Marcus, whose heart pounded against his rib cage like an animal clawing to free itself from a trap. Then it came to him. The walking stick! He still clutched the empty sheath in his fist.

"Ignite!" he shouted. The tip of the wooden staff burst into flame, and the flame quickly swelled into a roaring ball of fire. "No, no! Too much fire!" Marcus cried.

Bryn shrank back, shielding itself from the flame with its arm. The heat was so intense Marcus threw the staff away from him to prevent getting burned. Once separated from Marcus's hand, the flame withered and died.

Bryn immediately sprung forward, and Marcus braced himself for the attack. But just as Bryn advanced, it was thrown back, sprawling on the ground and whimpering like a frightened child.

Marcus spun round to see what force had repelled the attack and found himself gazing up into a face hidden by a dark, hooded robe covering its wearer from head to toe.

Bryn did not wait for a second blow. The creature fled on all fours, disappearing into the ever-darkening night of the canyon.

Marcus shook so hard with fright, his knees rapped together. The cloaked stranger stooped forward and picked up the blade with the eagle's head. He held it out to Marcus. "Yours?" he asked. Marcus accepted it meekly and replaced the sword in the now blackened sheath. "You are brave," the stranger continued, "but you would have been eaten alive."

Xerxes trembled in Marcus's hand. "What nerve, lighting *me* on fire!" he scolded angrily. Marcus tried to ignore the bird's complaint. His attention was focused on the man who had appeared seemingly out of nowhere.

The stranger knelt beside Kelvin and laid his ear against the boy's chest. "He is breathing. The Groc must have given him some sort of sedative. He will wake soon. Perhaps an hour or two."

"Groc?" asked Marcus.

"That thing you just encountered, the changeling. Grocs are cunning creatures that take whatever form suits them—if it will get them a meal. I'm surprised he attacked in daylight, however. Grocs are usually nocturnal. They hunt at night."

Marcus shuddered, thinking of what might have been his fate had this man not arrived when he had. "How did you . . . where did you come from all of a sudden like that?" he asked.

The man pointed to the top of the canyon. Marcus realized that as hard as it was to believe, he must have jumped from up there. This was the shadow that had been following them.

"You saved my life and the life of my friend," Marcus continued. "How can I ever repay you?"

"No payment is required," the stranger replied.

"At least tell me your name."

The stranger turned toward Marcus. "My name is Jayson," he said.

Grasping his hood with his hands, Jayson pulled it back, revealing a head of woolly black hair and catlike eyes as gray as the clouds over a stormy sea. Marcus gasped involuntarily. Their rescuer wasn't human—at least not completely human. Marcus had never seen a half-breed Agoran before.

Thirteen

arcus! Kelvin!"

The happy shouts of four boys reverberated against the canyon walls. It was a welcome sound, almost as welcome as the sight of them running through the narrow passage. Marcus, who had just helped Kelvin onto his feet after the Groc's paralyzing potion began to wear off, nearly fell on his backside when Tristan Tether tackled him.

"We nearly gave you up for dead!" teased Tristan, the yellow scarf from the ceremony still tied around his neck. "I ran into Clovis holding his nose at the entrance of the canyon. We would have caught up with you sooner, but look what we found."

In the company of Tristan and Clovis were the other two boys from Quendel.

Jerrid Zwelger picked a speck of dust from his new leather satchel and flicked it away. "When we hadn't seen you two by this morning," he said, "we imagined the worst."

Zody Smythe's freckled face broke into a grin as he gave a timid laugh. "We thought you got eaten!"

"That is, until we saw that snake carcass," added Jerrid, coolly. "I only know one person who can wield a death blow with a dagger."

Quick as a flash, Jerrid snatched Kelvin's dagger from its sheath and brandished it in the air. Kelvin, who was still recovering from his paralysis, did not resist. "To Kelvin Archer!" shouted Jerrid. He raised the dagger above his head and let out a loud whoop. The other boys echoed it, filling the canyon with a strange music.

When the noise died down, Kelvin accepted his dagger back from Jerrid. He wobbled unsteadily. Marcus handed Kelvin the walking stick, and Kelvin leaned against it gratefully. Jerrid nudged Zody with his elbow as the two exchanged derisive glances.

"Looks like Marcus brought along a little friend for company," Jerrid said, snickering.

Marcus held his anger in check, though he dreaded the mockery he would have to endure once Jerrid learned that Kelvin had nearly lost his life because of him.

"Marcus and I fought the snake together," Kelvin said. "We had a run-in with a Groc, as well."

"A Groc!" Suddenly the boys were all ears.

"Did you kill it?" asked Tristan.

"Where's the body?" prodded Zody.

"Did you escape?" asked Clovis.

"They're alive, aren't they, brain-boy?" replied Jerrid, his voice thick with cynicism. Clovis cast his eyes downward, ashamed.

Tristan stepped forward. "Kelvin must have fought him off," he said, patting Clovis on the shoulder. "How did you manage?"

To Marcus's relief, Kelvin said nothing of Marcus's role in bringing the Groc into their company. In fact, it seemed he would say nothing at all.

Marcus spoke up. "Actually, we have Jayson to thank for saving us."

"Who's Jayson?" Jerrid asked.

Having gone unnoticed by the excited boys, Jayson now stepped forward. His broad shoulders and grave countenance gave an air of nobility, though his cloak was torn and coated in moist earth. "It is my pleasure to meet you all," he said.

There was an awkward silence as the boys gaped at the stranger. They seemed particularly riveted to his eyes. Marcus noted again how strange they looked, their pupils narrow slits like a cat's, and pale—the color of wet clay on a potter's wheel. The silence was broken, however, when Jerrid extended his hand. Jayson took it firmly.

"Come on, then!" said Jerrid. "We should reach Noam by nightfall. Once there we'll head to the nearest tavern and celebrate the success of the first leg of our journey."

Kelvin and the others followed Jerrid around the next bend in the passage, but Marcus held back. He glanced apprehensively behind and above. A shiver crawled up his spine, and as he hurried to catch up to his companions, he could not shake the feeling that someone or something still lurked in the shadows.

Fourteen

Daylight was fast receding as two wooden skiffs reached Illian Bay. One passenger from each boat stepped into the shallow waves to heave their crafts onto shore—an easy task for brutes such as these. If not for their faces, pockmarked and malformed as they were, they might have passed for rather sizable humans. The Mardoks were taller and vastly broader than their human leader, and yet they obeyed him unquestioningly.

Under any other circumstances, Arik would have preferred to work alone. But despite his distaste for subhumans, the man/beast Mardoks were both physically strong and mentally inferior—the makings of an effective and compliant crew.

A quick-tempered man with hair as red as flame, Arik stepped from his boat while still in the shallows and strode purposely toward drier land. He had waited so long for this moment—sacrificed so much—and though years of ambition and vengeance had hardened him, he reveled at feeling Imaness beneath his feet once again.

Once the boats were secure, the remaining Mardoks stepped onto the wet sand carrying two small crates and torches. Arik called to them in short, gruff commands. "Quickly now! Scan every inch! Don't let a twig or leaf escape your eyes!"

While the seven Mardoks scurried along the forest's border, Arik inspected the beach. Though partially eroded from the tide, evidence of an earlier visitor was still apparent. A trail of footprints crisscrossed where forest and beach met, finally disappearing into a dense patch of undergrowth.

"Here!" he shouted. The adrenaline surged in his veins. He breathed deeply, and the exhilaration of the moment made his skin tingle. He lifted his hand to the side of his face and rubbed the raw, newly healed scar that covered the space his left ear had once occupied. Days had passed, yet it ached even now. How he longed for a chance to avenge his loss.

The Mardoks hurried to the spot. Arik tugged at branches and vines, commanding the others to do the same. One Mardok lit its torch and flourished it at the trees. "Let's burn our way through!" it shouted, lighting a branch aflame.

"You fool!" shouted Arik. Moving quickly, he snapped off the burning limb and struck the culprit with it. The creature screamed in pain, its face singed from the flame.

"Fire will only alert our enemy to our presence, not to mention every other person who lives on this wretched island!" Arik gestured toward the footprints in the sand. "The access is here! Find it now, or I will leave you all here to die!"

They tried to breach the foliage with renewed vigor. Then for one of the Mardoks, the forest gave way. Arik pushed the beast aside and gazed at the narrow opening with satisfaction. A seeming lifetime of ambitions and designs were culminating in this moment. But there was no time for pride: Soon they had to be on the other side of the island.

Arik ordered the crates to be brought to him. He reached into one and removed a small gray bird with a yellow band around its leg. Once released, the bird took flight, soaring into the sky and disappearing over the tops of the trees.

Fifteen

It was nearing nightfall by the time Marcus and company emerged from Vrystal Canyon. Below them the Village of Noam spread out like a vast, green carpet dotted here and there by low hillsides. Huts made of stone were scattered about at random, each with a thin plume of smoke curling up from a squat chimney. About a mile from the canyon was a cluster of a dozen or more identical wooden structures and a water well, which the boys guessed was the village square.

"Finally, a place where I can get a suitable meal," said Jerrid, surveying the valley with an approving nod. "Zody, take my pack while I make my way down."

"Don't do it, Zody," said Tristan, passing the other boys to start down the hill. Calling over his shoulder, he added, "He's not a pack animal, Jerrid!"

"But I don't mind. Really." Zody took Jerrid's pack and slung it over his shoulder, opposite his own pack. Then he followed Jerrid down the steep slope. Near the bottom, Zody slipped on some loose soil, slid into Jerrid nearly knocking him off balance, and endured a berating from his friend for being clumsy. Marcus watched the scene from above. He couldn't help but chuckle a little.

"Those two are an odd pair," said Jayson, the mysterious savior who had rescued Kelvin and Marcus from the jaws of the hungry Groc.

Kelvin, still a bit shaky from his earlier encounter, leaned against a nearby tree stump and took a long swig from his water skin. "No more odd than some of us," he said.

Ignoring Kelvin, Jayson directed his comments to Marcus. "Noam has several satisfactory inns, but I recommend the one on the north side of the fountain," he said, pointing. "You'll find a warm bed and excellent service there."

"You're not staying with us?" Marcus asked. Though their journey together had been a short one, he felt safer in the company of the man in the black cloak. He was sure Kelvin agreed. To his dismay, however, Kelvin offered neither thanks nor a request for Jayson to stay with them.

"But you need a place to rest, too," Marcus said. "Why don't you come with us?"

Kelvin crossed his arms. His face wore an impatient expression.

"I hesitated to ask earlier," said Jayson, nodding toward the other boys who had nearly reached the bottom of the slope that led to the village, "but what were two lads like yourselves doing alone in Groc territory?"

Kelvin straightened himself as best he could and squared his shoulders. "We're on a quest."

"What sort of quest?"

"We are on a long journey and will be men upon our return."

"Men?" Jayson laughed. "Why, you are only boys! If I hadn't come along, you both would be Groc droppings by now."

Kelvin's jaw tightened, and Marcus sensed for the first time a hint of anger in his companion. "I admit that I was taken by surprise," said Kelvin. "But Marcus and I would have killed the creature if you had not interfered."

Jayson raised a skeptical eyebrow at Kelvin. "Is that so?" he said, still smiling. "Grocs do not generally give up as easily as that one did. So how, pray tell, would you have killed it? You were unconscious, and Marcus was paralyzed with fear."

Kelvin's hand went to his dagger, and for a moment Marcus feared he would draw it. "I assure you, sir," Kelvin answered, his eyes locked on Jayson's with an icy glare, "we do not require your protection—or your companionship."

"Afraid I'll eat you in your sleep, like that Groc?" asked Jayson, obviously taking pleasure in provoking Kelvin.

"Please," Marcus said, interrupting. "We're all hungry and tired. Let's go down and get something to eat."

Marcus disagreed with Kelvin. He was certain that the Groc would have killed them both if not for Jayson's chance appearance. The only way to truly thank Jayson for saving their lives was to invite him to join them for supper.

"On second thought, I will join you both," Jayson replied with a smirk. "And Kelvin, you have nothing to fear from me. Agorans don't much care for human flesh. Too gamey."

Jayson moved on toward the village below. Marcus hurried down the slope after him, hoping Kelvin would follow. He did not look back, but to his relief, he soon heard his footsteps following behind.

Sixteen

The rooms at the Noamish inn proved to be plain yet suitable. After their two-day trek through the Black Forest and Vrystal Canyon, the boys longed for a good meal and comfortable bed.

After cleaning themselves in tubs of steaming water, they convened in the guest hall where they feasted on roast duck and stewed cabbage. With their stomachs filled, they warmed themselves by the wide granite hearth and boasted to one another of their adventures so far. One by one, each boy excused himself for the evening. By midnight only Jayson and Marcus remained—along with Jerrid Zwelger, who had laid his head on the table and fallen asleep.

Marcus placed his satchel between his head and the back of his chair. His eyes felt heavy, but the crackle and warmth of the fire held him as though in a trance. His thoughts turned to Zyll's cottage, small but comfortable and perfectly suited to their needs. He recalled his old master. Marcus considered himself fortunate to have had such a benevolent guardian, as his upbringing was not usual for orphans. That he would be brought up an apprentice, sent to school, and allowed to embark on a quest were privileges customarily reserved only for sons.

Jayson joined Marcus beside the fire and placed his feet on the hearth. The maidservant offered him a full tankard of ale, which he downed in a single swallow.

"Why don't you just bring me the whole cask?" he suggested, passing the empty tankard back to the maid. She curtsied and hurried from the room. Jayson stretched his legs out before him and wriggled his bare feet in front of the fire.

"That's one ugly bag," he said, poking Marcus's satchel with his finger. "It looks like a half-eaten carcass."

Marcus placed the satchel beneath his chair. Then he leaned forward to warm his hands near the fire. He was glad he had left Xerxes in his room, or he might have had to endure even more ridicule.

"So tell me more about this quest you are on," said Jayson.

"We're supposed to find something and bring it back to our village," Marcus answered.

"What something?"

"A stone." Marcus spoke cautiously, forming the words on his lips as if they were a secret, the revelation of which might release some terrible curse.

The maidservant returned, straining under the weight of the wooden keg she carried. When she came to the hearth, she set it down and wiped her hands on her apron.

"Now that's more like it!" said Jayson, pulling off the lid and lifting it to his lips with both hands. The servant just shook her head and began clearing the table, careful not to disturb the boy who was using it as a pillow.

Jayson set down the keg and wiped his mouth with his sleeve. "What sort of stone is worth sending six children on such a dangerous quest?"

Marcus bristled at being called a child, but he tried not to show it. "Some say it is a magical stone," he said.

"A magical stone? Just what kind of magic does this stone possess?"

"I'm not sure, really," Marcus explained. "I've heard a rumor that it has the power to destroy kingdoms and raise them up again."

Jayson's eyes gazed into the flames as though his mind were drifting to a distant place. "Such a power would be useful in times like these," he said more to himself than to Marcus. Jayson's eyes flashed with energy. He broke from the hypnotic fire and turned back to his ale. "So where is this magic stone?"

"No one knows," said Marcus. "That's why we've come to Noam, to study the writings in the library. Maybe there we'll find more information."

"The library, eh? You could be there for months and never find what you're looking for." Jayson swayed unsteadily before he leveled off. The ale was beginning to work a magic of its own upon him. "I am somewhat familiar with the history of these parts. Tell me its name," he continued. "Perhaps I've heard of it. It has a name, hasn't it?"

Marcus chewed his lower lip, unsure if he should divulge such information. What if the stone was valuable? What if Jayson did know of it and took it for himself? Would Marcus's quest be a failure? He studied Jayson's face for a long moment, searching for some justification of his mistrust. He found none.

"It has a name," Marcus answered, lowering his voice. "We seek the Rock of Ivanore."

There was a silent pause, and for a moment Marcus thought he saw a hint of recognition pass through Jayson's eyes. Then, to Marcus's surprise, Jayson threw back his head and roared with laughter. This continued for several minutes. Each time it seemed that Jayson had gotten control of himself, his laughter began anew. It was a good five minutes before he regained his composure, at which point he downed the remaining contents of his keg in its entirety.

"Why are you laughing?" Marcus asked defensively.

A wide grin spread across Jayson's face. "You seek the Rock of Ivanore? What village, may I ask, has sent you on this grand adventure?"

"Quendel," answered Marcus. "East of the Jeweled Mountains."

Jayson's grin widened even more. "Quendel. Yes, I know that place. And I suppose it was that old wizard of theirs, Zyll, who put you up to it, eh?"

Marcus nodded. He was quite perplexed now. How did Jayson know Zyll? Marcus had never seen Jayson in the village before. It must have been before Marcus was old enough to remember.

Jayson glanced toward the table where Jerrid still lay unmoving, then leaned close to Marcus, dropping his voice to just above a whisper. "Do you know why I laugh, Marcus? I laugh because what Zyll has sent you to find isn't magic at all. It isn't even a stone."

"Then you've heard of it?" asked Marcus, filled with sudden optimism.

"I should hope so!" said Jayson, stifling another laugh. "Because *I am* the Rock of Ivanore!"

Seventeen

ayson clasped his hands together and stared past the now-dying embers. A sudden melancholy came over him. Whether it was the effects of the ale setting in or the memories, Marcus wasn't sure.

"Ivanore is my wife," Jayson said.

A log in the fireplace broke in two, the shower of spark and ash resounding through the silence as though a tree had been felled. The only other sound in the room was Jerrid's occasional shifting upon the table. Marcus was filled with questions. He spoke cautiously.

"Isn't it against the law for humans to marry . . . your kind?"

Jayson's eyes were fixed on the fire. "I'm only half Agoran," he said spitefully, although the edge in his voice

softened as he continued. "We were wed in secret. Her
father had forbidden her to marry me, but we were young,
in love, and nothing and no one could separate us—or so
we thought."

Jayson's gaze drew inward as if observing some distant
memory. He did not see the embers now, or anything
around him. He saw her. He saw Ivanore. Marcus was
sure of it.

"She called me her rock because I was strong," Jayson
continued. "I stood up to her father, vowing to protect her
at any cost. And we were happy for a time. Until . . ." His
voice broke off. He raised his hand and ran it through his
disheveled hair. The expression on his face grew anxious.

"Until what?" Marcus coaxed gently. "What happened
to her?"

Jayson now turned his gaze on Marcus. His eyes were
vacant, as though they did not recognize him, but the
emptiness was fleeting. "In time her father's soldiers discovered our location," he said. "I was exiled. The last I
saw of my Ivanore, she was standing atop the cliffs of
Dokur watching me sail away shackled to the mast of her
father's ship. That was nearly fifteen years ago."

Marcus's interest intensified. "Exiled? But why?" he
asked, appalled.

"Isn't the answer obvious?" said Jayson bitterly, holding his clawed fingers to his face. "He did not want me to
pollute his daughter with my impure blood. Since then
not a day—not an hour!—has passed that I have not
thought of them and vowed one day to return."

Jayson rose to his feet. "The hour is late. I must rest for a bit before I continue my journey. I will be leaving at sunrise."

"Is that where you're going, back to Dokur? To Ivanore?" asked Marcus, eager to hear more. It seemed to him that Jayson was a mystery waiting to be solved.

Jayson walked across the room to the staircase, his shoulders hunched as though carrying an unseen burden.

"Yes," he replied, pausing on the bottom step. He stared ahead and did not speak for several moments. He drew a deep and troubled breath, and Marcus expected him to speak again. Instead he continued up the stairs, saying nothing. Marcus was alone with so many questions left unanswered.

THE SEARCH FOR TRUTH

Eighteen

The next morning Marcus awoke to the sound of a rooster crowing, ushering in the new day. He was accustomed to waking at that hour since he was responsible for milking Zyll's goat and gathering eggs for breakfast. As an orphan, it was his duty to tend to the general chores of the cottage. Thus, while all the other children in Quendel were still tucked snugly in their beds, he was up sweeping out the chimney, or scraping ice from the well, or darning stockings. So on this morning when the cock crowed, he awoke with a start as his companions slept on.

Remembering his conversation with Jayson the night before, he quickly pulled on his clothes and hurried outside. He found Jayson in the square filling his water skin at the well.

"Jayson!" Marcus called out. Jayson turned and pulled the hood of his cloak off his head.

"Marcus, what are you doing up at this ungodly hour of the day?"

"You're not leaving, are you?"

"I've several days' walking still ahead of me to reach Dokur, so I'd better get on with it."

"You're going to Ivanore," said Marcus.

"Yes, if all goes well. I don't know what sort of reception I'll have when I get there. At the very least, I expect to be exiled all over again."

Marcus shivered from the brisk morning air. He had left his cape back at the inn. "Why go at all then?" he asked, rubbing his hands together to stay warm. "Why not send word to your wife and have her meet you *here*?"

"I bear an important message for Lord Fredric, her father. The fate of Imaness rests on delivering it in time."

"Then let us come with you."

"That's enough, Marcus!"

Jayson's tone was severe, but immediately his countenance softened. He replaced the plug in his water skin and slung it across his back. "I should not have told you what I did last night," he said apologetically. "I'm afraid the ale got the better of me. You mustn't tell the others."

"But why?" said Marcus. "We came here to find *you*. How can you allow us to continue our quest in vain?"

"Your quest is not in vain," Jayson spoke in earnest now. "If Zyll wants you to bring the Rock of Ivanore back to Quendel, then I should be obliged to accompany you there, but I must first go to Dokur. If I am discovered, I will be arrested and perhaps killed. No one must know I am here until I have safely delivered my message. Will you keep my secret for me?"

Marcus replied quickly. "I promise," he said.

Jayson smiled with relief. "Thank you. And I promise that I will rejoin you in one week's time."

"Where will we meet?"

"Follow the main road toward Dokur. Stay in the village there. I will find you." Jayson pulled his hood over his head and began walking away.

"And what will I tell the others?" Marcus called out after him.

Jayson answered without turning around. "Tell them I said the stone you are seeking may be in those parts. Let your search carry you along."

Jayson's form disappeared behind a stable just beyond the border of the town square. Marcus turned and hurried back to the inn. He wondered how he would manage to keep such a secret from Kelvin and the others for so long. But then again, he had given his word, and by withholding Jayson's identity, his successful quest might be better assured. He would reveal the truth later, of course, after Jayson had delivered his message. Then he and the other boys would return to Quendel in triumph.

Nineteen

Jerrid Zwelger flung off his covers and cursed under his breath. The sight of Marcus's empty bed sent a jolt of adrenaline through him that immediately chased any remnants of sleep from his brain and body. The chill morning air bit into his lungs as he took his first breaths unprotected by the heavy, woolen blanket that had covered him during the night.

He had gone to bed long after everyone else had retired for the night. After supper he had laid his head on the table and fallen asleep. He guessed it was well past midnight when he had awakened and inadvertently overheard a private conversation between Marcus and Jayson. He had been about to make it known that he was awake and excuse himself from the room when he heard Jayson utter a statement that made his blood run hot.

Jayson, the Rock of Ivanore? Could it be?

Jerrid remained motionless on the table and listened intently as Jayson spoke of a secret marriage and exile. After Jayson and Marcus went upstairs and the embers in the hearth had cooled, Jerrid sat with his face in his hands, turning Jayson's words over and over in his mind.

Zyll had given six boys a charge to retrieve the Rock of Ivanore and bring it back to Quendel. In keeping with tradition, those who returned from their quests in triumph received the greatest of honors and rewards. Those who failed were destined to a life of mediocrity and shame.

Jerrid's father had never missed an opportunity to remind his son of his own quest many years earlier. "I was one of nine," he always began in his grating, pompous voice. "Quendel had a different master then, much more clever than Zyll. We were to slay a Cyclops and bring back its eye. We found him in the Caverns of Feolina, in the southern mountains. It was a young one, probably strayed from its herd. We surrounded him and closed in for the kill. Bartholomew Tendall was to fire the first arrow, but he was nervous. He hesitated—and the beast turned on him in a rage."

Here his father always curved his fingers as though they were claws and snarled like a wild animal. "One swipe and poor Tendall lay in pieces on the ground. The moment I saw him I knew what must be done. I flung myself upon the monster's back and slit its throat with my knife. The other boys gave me the honor of bearing home the eye."

A turn, a sweep of the arm, a pushing out of the chest as he relived that moment of glory from so many years ago. Surely no less glory awaited his son if he were to return to Quendel with the mystery of the Rock of Ivanore solved and in his possession.

But as his eyes blinked in the morning rays that escaped through the slats of the inn's low roof, Jerrid knew that his chance at such glory had slipped from his fingers.

Jerrid hurried down the stairs and through the dining hall where the innkeeper was just preparing the morning meal. He dashed out the front door and ran toward the town square. He was out of breath when he met Marcus walking toward him, shivering from the cold.

"Where is he?" demanded Jerrid, white wisps of warm breath curling up from his mouth and nose.

Marcus drew his eyebrows together and breathed into his cupped hands. "Who?"

"Jayson! Has he gone?"

Marcus nodded and continued past Jerrid into the inn. The smell of smoked ham and eggs wafted through the door. Jerrid's stomach rumbled inside of him, but his thoughts were not on his hunger. He ran past the fountain and on to the edge of the village. He searched the horizon for the dark cloak, but he could see it nowhere. How long had Jayson been gone, he wondered. Minutes? Hours? And to where?

Dokur!

But Dokur was several days' journey from Noam. If I leave now and travel quickly, Jerrid thought, I could catch up with Jayson by noon. But how could he coax Jayson to return with him to Quendel? And what if he was wrong?

Jerrid shivered, and he realized that he had left the inn dressed only in his nightshirt. His feet, bare on the cobblestone, felt like blocks of ice. He would return to the inn, he decided. They had all agreed to pay a visit to the library, and Jerrid thought he just might find some useful information there. He would try to get more information from Marcus later. Then he'd leave—maybe while the other boys ate lunch. By the time they realized he was gone, he would be hours into his journey. The next time he'd see them would be as he greeted them on the day they returned empty-handed to Quendel.

Twenty

The Noamish Library was the oldest and largest of its kind on the Isle of Imaness. It was the tallest building in Noam, tall enough for two full-grown men to stand on one another's shoulders and still not touch the roof. The arched entryway was intricately carved with graceful curved markings—runes from a language unfamiliar to the boys.

Tristan Tether put his nose up to the door and squinted. "I can't make it out. Just a bunch of gibberish."

Jerrid Zwelger grabbed the scarf around Tristan's neck and pulled him out of the way. He peered at the door, ignoring Tristan's hostile glare. "It's in the ancient tongue, that's why!"

"Can you read it?" asked Zody, hovering closely behind Jerrid.

"What a stupid question. Of course I can't!" said Jerrid. "None of us can. Only Zyll still knows how."

Clovis cleared his throat, and suddenly all eyes were on him. "His apprentice should be able to read it," he said.

Marcus felt his face grow flush. Kelvin, who was standing beside him, gave him a nudge. "Go on, apprentice," he said. "Give it a try."

Marcus stepped up to the door and read the markings, slowly mouthing out the syllables. "*Inil camru obraith os belu.*" As he struggled to think of the correct translation, he wished he had brought Xerxes with him to help instead of leaving the walking stick in his room. Remember your studies, he thought to himself. Remember the tomes of the ancients!

He closed his eyes and tried to picture in his mind the characters scrawled on the brittle, yellow pages of Zyll's books. He had often taken them from the shelves, blown dust from their covers, and laid them on the table to read. It was true that Marcus had found the study of language dull, but now he wished that he had seen the value in it.

He opened his eyes and read the words once more. As he gazed at the letters, it was as if they transformed themselves before his eyes. "Your quest," he read slowly, "begins behind these doors."

He was quite pleased with himself and waited for the praise he felt he deserved, but no thanks or appreciation was offered.

Marcus reached forward and gave the door a gentle shove. It opened as easily as if it were a curtain of silk, opening on silent hinges. As he stepped over the threshold, he felt as though he were entering a new world. Shelves laden with books and scrolls reached floor to ceiling. The smell of dust and leather let off an acrid perfume. There were no windows. The only light in the room emanated from oil lamps suspended from the high wooden beams crossing it above.

Directly in front of them stood a tall desk made of dark wood. From it, a lean, pointy-faced man glared down at them over the rims of his silver spectacles.

"Not open!" he screeched in a forced whisper. "Not open today!"

"The door was unlocked," Marcus stammered. "We've come to find—"

The librarian shook a long bony finger in the direction of the door. "Can't you read?"

"Yes," answered Marcus. "But—"

The librarian leaned over the desk and eyed Marcus with obvious contempt. "If you can read you should have known we are closed today, for I put the sign up myself."

This time it was Kelvin who responded. "There's no sign on the door but the one engraved on it."

"What! No sign?"

The librarian climbed down from his perch and hobbled over to the door. He stepped outside and glanced at the door. He returned to the desk, grumbling. "I put up that sign myself! Someone has stolen it! Very well," he said, "but make it quick! I have a luncheon at noon."

Marcus and the other boys craned their necks as they took in the vastness of the library. With so many volumes to choose from, how would they ever find what they were looking for, especially since they didn't really know *what* they were looking for?

The librarian seemed to sense their confusion. Once again he got down from the desk. He started up a narrow aisle and motioned for the boys to follow. "What's your topic?" he asked curtly. His voice sliced through the cavernous room like a hatchet.

"The Rock of Ivanore," answered Marcus.

The librarian turned and scrutinized them through narrowed eyes.

"What do you want with her?" he said suspiciously.

"Her?" asked the boys, bewildered. Marcus felt as though the secret he bore must be evident on his face, but no one looked at him.

The librarian continued. "What do you want with Ivanore?"

Kelvin spoke for the group. "We are on a quest to find the Rock of Ivanore," he said, "only we don't know where to find it."

"I've never heard of a *rock* of Ivanore," continued the librarian. "But there isn't a soul in these parts that doesn't know of Lady Ivanore."

"Lady?"

The librarian started down the aisle again. He turned one corner and another. Finally the librarian stopped beside a wide table made of the same dark wood as his desk and polished to a high sheen.

"Wait here," he said and disappeared down another aisle. Several minutes passed before he returned bearing a large leather book, which he laid carefully upon the table. Brushing the dust from it with his shirtsleeve, he read its title aloud: "*The Recent History of the Isle of Imaness,* compiled by Enarin Blotch and Cloret Snidely," he said proudly, as though the work had been his own. "You'll find what you need here. When you are finished, leave it on the table. I'll re-shelve it after you have left, which," he added, "I expect you'll do before noon!"

The librarian wandered away down yet another aisle, leaving the boys alone with the massive volume. At first they all just stared at it. Kelvin flipped through several pages but found nothing of interest.

"Try the index," Zody suggested.

"Good thinking," said Kelvin, turning to the last page and drawing a finger along the list of names and locations. "Here it is," he said at last. "Ivanore of Dokur, page 572." He turned to the correct page. The faces of the others hovered over his shoulder as he read:

IVANORE OF DOKUR – Daughter of Lord Fredric Isley, ruler of the province of Dokur, having dwelt in the Fortress of Dokur until her sixteenth year, at which time she was kidnapped and forced to marry an Agoran half-breed. For one year, her whereabouts were unknown, but upon the capture and exile of the culprit, Ivanore returned home. Within days of her return, however, she disappeared again. It has been suspected that the Agoran's sup-

porters took her to avenge him, but such claims have gone largely unsubstantiated. From the day of her disappearance, there have been no reports of her. While some claim she is being held captive in the kingdom of Hestoria on the mainland, others believe she died a tragic death long ago.

Kelvin closed the book.

"So where does this leave us?" asked Zody.

"Nowhere," said Clovis, his shoulders drooping with disappointment.

"One measly paragraph," complained Tristan. "So Ivanore is some dead woman. I knew Zyll was crazy sending us on this quest."

Discouragement permeated the air around the table. Marcus felt a twinge of guilt that he had pledged to keep Jayson's true identity secret when his friends so desperately wanted to succeed. He thought of what the book had said, that Ivanore had been kidnapped, possibly murdered. Had Jayson lied to him? And if so, would it hurt to tell the other boys of his plan? No, Marcus reassured himself. I gave my word.

"We know one thing," Marcus said aloud. All eyes turned to him. "We know she came from Dokur."

"So?" said Tristan.

"So," Kelvin said, "we go to Dokur."

Twenty-one

Marcus stepped out of the library and shielded his eyes from the bright afternoon sun. It was a brisk day despite the clear skies, and he felt inclined to trade his cape for a heavy blanket and a bowl of hot soup. He and the other boys made their way toward the inn. There was a commotion outside as they approached. The Noamish innkeeper was in a heated conversation with a redheaded man. Six other men stood beside him. They were much taller than the first, however, and twice as broad. No, not men, thought Marcus. A second look and he knew immediately what they were: Mardoks!

"I've told you all I know!" the innkeeper shouted impatiently. "He is not here! Now be gone with you!"

Tristan leaned close to Marcus and whispered. "Who are those fellows? I've never seen men so big and hairy before."

"Mardoks," said Marcus. "They're Hestorian assassins—inhumans."

"How do you know about assassins?"

"Zyll has told me stories about them. We should be careful."

Tristan's voice grew even softer. "Hestoria is on the mainland. What are they doing here?"

Marcus did not know, but he wanted to find out.

"I hope they haven't spoiled our lunch," said Jerrid, pushing past the other boys. "We should go in before the soup gets cold."

Kelvin grasped Jerrid's shoulder and held him back. "This isn't right," he said. His voice was low as though he sensed some danger. "We should go back to the library 'til they've gone."

There was a silent consensus as the boys hurried back toward the library. Even Jerrid and Zody reluctantly agreed that Kelvin might be right. One by one, they slipped through the library door, but before Marcus reached the threshold, a voice stopped him.

"You there!" The voice was deep and imposing. Marcus turned hesitantly. The man addressing him was the same man who had been arguing with the innkeeper. "Come here, boy," he commanded.

As Marcus approached, the man scrutinized him with dark, deeply set eyes. His left ear was missing, the jagged wound partially hidden by several days' growth of whiskers. "You're not a Noam," he said. "Where are you from?"

"Quendel, sir."

"Quendel? Is that north of here?"

"No, sir," answered Marcus, trying not to stare at the man's injury. "East of the mountains, through the pass."

The man arched his eyebrows.

"I see," he said. "Then perhaps you can help me."

Marcus nervously shifted his weight from one foot to the other.

"My name is Arik," the man continued. "I'm looking for a man who wears a black cloak—a half-breed. There is a bounty on his head."

Marcus glanced up into Arik's face. "Bounty? Has he committed a crime?" he asked.

Arik leaned forward until his face was mere inches from Marcus's. Their eyes met, and the man held his gaze like a magnet to iron. "He has something that belongs to me," he said, lowering his voice. "Have you seen such a man?"

Marcus shook his head. "No," he said. "No one like that."

Arik straightened himself and sighed with mock disappointment. He waved a hand in the direction of his companions. "Perhaps you haven't," he said, "but this creature has."

One of the Mardoks shoved a young boy forward. His hands were bound with ropes, and the other Mardoks laughed as he stumbled forward. Marcus instantly recognized him as Bryn, the Groc that had nearly killed Kelvin in Vrystal Canyon.

Arik spoke again. "Don't be fooled. This *child* is a monster in disguise. I was fortunate to have captured it, but not before it killed one of my men. It claims that a man in a black cloak attacked him only yesterday. What's more, the beast says the man was not alone." He walked over to Bryn and forcefully pulled up the child's chin. "Is this one of the boys you saw yesterday?"

Bryn stared forward with defiant eyes. Arik slapped him across the face, nearly knocking him to the ground. "Answer me or you will be severely punished!"

Marcus held his breath. He could not, however, keep his heart from racing. What would happen if Bryn identified him?

Bryn winced in pain and then shook his head. "No," he said. "I have never seen that one before."

Arik lifted his hand to strike again, but Bryn curled his lips, revealing two rows of razor-sharp fangs. Arik dropped his hand, turning instead toward Marcus.

"Sorry to have troubled you," he said. "If you see the half-breed, tell him Arik is looking for him." As he turned to rejoin his men, Marcus called after him.

"And what will you do with him when you find him?"

This time Arik did not turn around. He stopped beside Bryn and glared at him with contempt. "The same that I will do to this creature." Arik looked back at Marcus. His lips twisted into a satisfied grin, and the scar on the side of his face contorted grotesquely. "I'll execute him, of course."

Arik turned to the Mardoks. "Search the village! Every door, every stone must be explored! And find me some horses!"

Arik and his assassins dispersed, leaving one behind to guard the Groc. This Mardok, however, seemed disinterested in his prisoner and wandered toward the tavern, leaving Bryn tied to the well. Marcus approached cautiously. As he did so, Bryn turned away, hiding his face with his arms. His shoulders trembled ever so slightly.

"Why didn't you tell them you recognized me?" asked Marcus.

At first Bryn ignored him, but after a moment he lifted his head. Marcus was shocked to see tears trickling down his cheeks.

"I hate you," said Bryn, "but I hate *him* even more." He held up his hands, and Marcus saw the raw patches on his wrists where the ropes had burned them. Bryn's lip began to quiver, and a new round of tears began to fall. Seeing him like this, it was difficult for Marcus to think of him as the fierce creature that had attacked him only yesterday.

"Thank you," Marcus offered.

"For what?" snapped Bryn.

"For your kindness in not giving me away."

"It wasn't kindness! I haven't eaten in three days! I would have finished off that Mardok in the canyon, but how was I to know there were so many of them not far behind?"

Marcus could see that Bryn's lips were cracked and parched from thirst. He took a bucket resting on the edge of the well and filled it with water. He held it up to Bryn's mouth. The Groc eyed him with suspicion but then greedily lapped up the water with an elongated tongue. When he had finished drinking, Bryn leaned back against the fountain, apparently satisfied.

"Thank you," he said meekly. "It is the first drink I've had in many days. And it will likely be my last since that man plans to kill me when he returns."

Marcus thought for a moment. He remembered what Jayson had told him about Grocs and their cunning and deception. Yet Bryn had protected Marcus from Arik. He owed him for that.

Keeping one eye on the back of the Mardok guard who had his head tucked in the tavern door, he worked quickly to untie Bryn's ropes. Once free, Bryn rubbed his injured wrists. Marcus thought he saw a slight smile on Bryn's lips, but then in a single swift moment, Bryn dashed across the courtyard and was gone.

Twenty-two

Marcus hurried toward the inn. He wanted to be alone. He needed time to think. But just as he reached the door, someone grabbed him from behind.

"What did that man want with you?" Kelvin demanded.

"Nothing," Marcus replied, trying not to sound anxious. "He's looking for someone—"

"A half-breed," said Kelvin.

The word caught Marcus off guard. "You heard him from inside the library?"

"He's looking for Jayson."

"No." Marcus forced a smile, but he suspected Kelvin could not be so easily fooled. "He was looking for someone else. I told him we couldn't help him."

"Half-breeds are rare," said Kelvin. "I've seen only one in my whole life, and I suspect it is the same one you have seen." His voice dropped to a whisper. "The book spoke of a half-breed who kidnapped Ivanore. Maybe it was Jayson."

Marcus thought about this. Kelvin could be right, and the truth troubled him. He was tempted to tell Kelvin all he knew about Jayson, but he dared not break his promise. Instead, he heard himself say, "Jayson would never do such a thing."

Kelvin's response was harsh. "How can you say that when we know nothing about him, nothing except that he saved us from being eaten by that disgusting Groc, he had supper with us, and now he's gone?"

"Will you betray him to Arik, then?" asked Marcus.

Kelvin recoiled at the accusation, as if it had stung him like a hornet. "I won't betray the man who saved my life. I am in his debt," he said. "But I must know the truth about him. Tell me what you know."

"There's nothing to tell." The deceit tasted bitter in Marcus's mouth. He tried to keep his gaze steady, but he could not, and he looked away.

"You're lying!" Kelvin grabbed Marcus by the shoulders and pinned him against the building wall. "I don't like liars," he said menacingly.

Marcus struggled to break free from Kelvin's grip. He wrapped his arms around Kelvin's neck and twisted with all his might. They collapsed on the ground, where they wrestled against each other's strength. Marcus was surprised to discover how equally matched they were in the struggle. At last Kelvin broke away.

"You aren't worth the trouble," he said. Then he spat on the ground and walked away.

Marcus waited until Kelvin had gone before he tried to stand. He felt weak and his legs wobbled beneath him. He touched the side of his head. Blood trickled from a small cut. Though he felt angry, he blamed himself for Kelvin's actions. He had lied to him, and Kelvin knew it. But though Kelvin meant well, Marcus was determined to keep the secret entrusted to him—at all costs.

He was about to return to the inn to wash, when a glimmer on the ground caught his eye. The sunlight reflected off something near his feet. He picked it up and turned it over in his hand. It was a stone, flat and triangular in shape. One edge was smooth and rounded while the other two were rough and uneven, as if the piece had been broken from a larger whole. It was translucent, like crystal, but clearer than any crystal he had ever seen. Its color was the palest green, or was it blue? It seemed a blend of both, just a hint of the color of the sea.

Marcus held it up by the leather cord on which it was strung. It seemed familiar to him somehow, and he realized that he had seen it once before, but only for a brief moment. It was Kelvin's pendant that he now held in his hand.

Marcus touched the wound on his temple and flinched from the pain. Kelvin doesn't understand that I have to keep my word, he told himself. He should have trusted me.

Marcus placed the leather cord around his neck and tucked the pendant inside his shirt. Then he hurried through the inn door and ran up the stairs to his room.

Twenty-three

Marcus shut the door of his room and closed his eyes in momentary relief. He wanted to be alone to sort out the many thoughts that were spinning inside his head.

Xerxes stood propped up in the corner, unmoved from the spot where Marcus had left him the night before. Xerxes' eyelids fluttered open, and he let out a soft squawk.

"Where have you been?" he said. "You missed our lesson this morning!"

"Not now, Xerxes," said Marcus, sitting on his cot.

"You look ill," said Xerxes. "Have you been eating that horrid stew I've been smelling all afternoon?"

Marcus laid his head on his satchel. "I think Jayson is in trouble," he said. He wanted to tell Xerxes everything—

about Jayson's secret, that he was Ivanore's husband come back to find her. But he had sworn an oath not to reveal it to anyone. "I met a man outside just now," he began cautiously. "I went to the library with the others to research the Rock of Ivanore—"

Xerxes interrupted him, his voice tinged with excitement. "What did you learn?"

"Ivanore is a woman," Marcus began, "the daughter of Dokur's sovereign."

"A woman?"

"The book claimed she was kidnapped many years ago and has not been seen since."

"Kidnapped by whom?"

Marcus hesitated. *If I tell Xerxes about the half-breed, he will surely think it was Jayson,* Marcus thought. Marcus tugged at a loose thread dangling from the frayed edge of his blanket.

"It didn't say," he lied.

"Well, did the book say anything about a rock?"

Marcus shook his head. He felt a pang of guilt for his deception but reassured himself that he was keeping his oath and that once Jayson had delivered his message, he would be free to tell Xerxes the truth.

A knock at the door startled him.

"Who is it?" called Marcus.

The door squeaked open, and Jerrid Zwelger stepped into the room. He was wearing his cloak and that annoying new satchel of his. *He's so anxious to get this quest over with,* thought Marcus, *he's probably come to hurry the rest of us along.*

"I thought I heard you talking to someone," said Jerrid, "but I see that you're alone."

"What do you want, Jerrid?"

"I'm looking for Jayson."

"He isn't here," Marcus answered without even trying to mask his irritation. "I told you before, he's gone."

Jerrid glanced at Marcus's exhausted, dirt-smeared face and quickly closed the door behind him. "Where has he gone?" Jerrid asked, almost in a whisper.

Marcus felt a strange uneasiness creeping into him as though a cold wind had blown over him. He looked toward the window expecting to find it open. It was shut tight. "I don't know," Marcus answered.

Jerrid took a step forward, closing the space between them. "Jayson didn't tell you why he was in such a hurry to leave, or where he was going?"

"No."

The lies came more freely now. Marcus felt driven to them, in fact, as though they were shielding him from some unseen danger.

Jerrid's eyes remained fixed on Marcus for several moments. "It's peculiar, don't you think, that Ivanore was kidnapped by a half-breed?" Jerrid said, as he turned to leave. "There should be a handsome reward for the villain."

Jerrid opened the door. He paused and said, "Jayson is a half-breed, isn't he?" Then he stepped into the hall and closed the door behind him.

Twenty-four

Once the sound of Jerrid's footsteps had faded away, Xerxes sprung back to life. "What's this about the half-breed?" he screeched.

Marcus tried to hush him. "Quiet! They'll hear you!"

"It's not me they'll hear!" Xerxes retorted. "I thought you said the book said nothing about who kidnapped Ivanore! And what does Jayson have to do with all this?"

"He's not responsible! He can't be!" Marcus dropped his face into his hands and moaned. "Besides, I swore an oath to protect his identity."

The muffled sound of voices drifted into the room through the closed window. Marcus went to it, opening it just a crack. Below him, in front of the inn, were Arik and his men.

"What's going on out there? Who is shouting?" demanded Xerxes.

"It's Arik, that awful man I started telling you about. He approached me earlier and asked if I had seen a half-breed. I'm certain he's looking for Jayson. Just a minute . . ."

Marcus drew a shallow breath and held it. As he forced himself to expel the air from his lungs, heat rose into his cheeks. "Jerrid is with them!" he said. "I can't make out what he is saying. He's pointing at this window!"

Arik turned his face upward to where Marcus watched from the window, and for a brief moment their eyes locked. Marcus turned quickly from the window.

"Jerrid's betrayed us!"

Marcus grabbed his satchel and hastily stuffed his belongings into it, and then he picked up Xerxes with his free hand. Last of all, he snatched up the key.

"Where are we going?" asked Xerxes. "We can't just leave! There are bills to be paid!"

Marcus threw open the door and descended the wooden staircase two steps at a time. When he reached the bottom, he paused beside the entrance and ventured a quick look outside.

"Arik is coming this way! We'll have to leave through the alley."

Marcus had just slipped through the kitchen door when Arik burst into the inn.

"Search the rooms!" he bellowed so loudly that Marcus could hear his voice through the exterior wall. "I want that boy alive!"

*   *   *

Gathered at the table in the inn's dining hall were Kelvin, Tristan, Zody, and Clovis. They had been discussing their earlier discovery at the library when Arik and the Mardoks stormed in. Arik strode across the room, drew his sword, and stabbed their table with it, leaving the sword standing upright from its center. The crowded dining room grew silent as all eyes turned to the center table.

"Tell me where he is, and I may spare your miserable lives," he said. "You there!"

Tristan struggled to swallow the lump of bread he had been chewing. His mouth had gone dry. "Me?" he said, tugging at his yellow scarf to loosen it somewhat.

"Where is the lad I spoke with this morning?"

"I haven't seen him in the last hour . . . sir."

Arik's attention turned toward Clovis. "I asked you where your companion is!" Arik's voice strained with frustration. Clovis stammered, unable to get even a word out. "Speak up, boy!" Arik shouted.

"M-my n-ose is b-bleeding." Indeed, Clovis's nose had begun to drip blood as if on command.

Disgusted, Arik raised his hand to strike him, but Tristan stood quickly, placing himself between Arik and Clovis.

"Don't touch him," said Tristan in a calm, steady voice that surprised them all. "Like the rest of us, he hasn't seen Marcus since this morning."

"I saw him half an hour ago."

Zody, who had been silent until now, was shaking like the last leaf on an autumn vine. Arik's sword had buried its point only inches from his plate.

"Quiet!" commanded Tristan, but the command had come too late.

Arik walked around the table and laid a heavy hand on Zody's quivering shoulder. "Go on," he said.

Perspiration coated Zody's freckled forehead and dripped into his eyes. "He was with Kelvin."

Arik removed his hand. Zody sighed with visible relief.

"And where is this Kelvin?"

The boys glanced about the room. Kelvin had been dining with them only moments before. Now he was nowhere to be seen.

Twenty-five

Marcus quickly made his way toward the back of the inn, where the alley crossed a narrow residential road. Noams pulled their handcarts laden with fruit, corn, and other goods, not bothering even to look up at the tall stranger. Marcus took a moment to catch his breath.

Xerxes clicked his beak. "Do you really think you can hide from those men? You're like a giant here!"

"I don't intend to hide!" snapped Marcus. The tension of the day's events was wearing on him. Suddenly a hand fell on his shoulder. He quickly turned and drew back, ready for a fight.

It was Kelvin. "I was in the dining hall when I saw you run out the back way. When Arik came in, I knew you were in trouble."

Seeing Kelvin's face was like a balm to Marcus's frayed nerves, but he was still angry about their scuffle. "Have you come to say good-bye?" asked Marcus sarcastically.

"I'm coming with you," answered Kelvin, patting the skin parcel tucked beneath his arm. There was no time for apologies now. Marcus glanced back toward the road. All they had to do was cross it and head out beyond the crags. The high boulders would make traveling more difficult, but they would also block them from Arik's view until they were a safe distance from Noam.

"We had better go before Arik's men decide to search the alley," said Kelvin.

"Too late!" Marcus cried.

Behind them two Mardoks shouted and began running toward them. Kelvin grabbed Marcus's arm and dragged him across the street toward the hills. Just as they reached the other side, the Mardoks emerged from the alley. Kelvin dove behind a grassy knoll and pulled Marcus down beside him.

"What are you doing?" hissed Marcus. "We can't stay here! They'll kill us!"

"Not today," said Kelvin, unwrapping the parcel to reveal a worn but sturdy crossbow and a dozen arrows. "I thought we might be needing these."

"Clovis's bow!" said Marcus.

Kelvin ran his hand admiringly down the length of the stock. "I'd trade my dagger for this any day."

"You can't take Clovis's only weapon!" snapped Marcus. "His father would kill him for losing it. Take it back and find something else!"

"There isn't time!"

In a single swift movement Kelvin got to his knees, lined an arrow in his sight, and let it fly. It pierced the first Mardok at the hip, crippling it with pain. Kelvin reached for another arrow, but the second Mardok jumped atop the knoll, bared his teeth, and growled. Kelvin held the bow at waist level and released the string. The arrow entered the creature's stomach and continued out its back, lodging itself in a passing wagon. The injured creature howled in agony and collapsed in a limp heap, dead.

Marcus nodded furiously. "All right. We'll just *borrow* it for awhile. Clovis will understand—I hope."

Kelvin grabbed Marcus and shoved him back toward the road. The wagoneer had stopped to investigate the arrow sticking out of his wagon.

"Get in!" shouted Kelvin. Marcus obeyed, heaving himself into the wagon bed just as Kelvin snatched up the reins.

"Hey! Wait!" the wagoneer called out, but Kelvin ignored the man's pleas. This was no time for manners.

"Uhta! Uhta!" Kelvin shouted. The horses lurched forward, nearly throwing Marcus out onto the road, but he managed to pull himself in and huddled beside a pile of animal skins as the wagon gathered speed.

He glanced over the side of the wagon just in time to see Arik run into the middle of the road. Marcus thought surely he would pursue them, but Arik just stood there watching them with hate-filled eyes. Marcus met his gaze. Neither he nor Arik looked away until they had long disappeared from each others' sights.

Twenty-six

Arik did not waste any time after watching his prize disappear in a stolen wagon. He turned on his heels and marched through the alley back into the inn. He announced his presence by grabbing Clovis by the hair and pulling him to his feet.

"Your friends have deserted you!" he shouted, not even attempting to hide his scorn. "They have gone to warn my enemy, but that is of no concern to me now." He threw Clovis toward the corner of the room, where the boy landed on his knees, whimpering in fear. His nose-bleed had slowed to a trickle by now.

Tristan hurried to Clovis's side. He untied his scarf and pinched Clovis's nose with it. "What do you want from us?" he demanded of Arik. "We don't know where they've gone!"

At the table, a Mardok grabbed Zody by the arm. The beast's massive fingers easily encircled the boy's slender limb. Though Zody struggled to free himself, he was no match for the Mardok's strength.

Arik raised the tip of his sword and tucked it just beneath Zody's chin. "I already know where they are going," he said. "The objective now is to get there before they do. And if I fail…" Arik quickly withdrew his blade, leaving a thin, shallow cut on Zody's chin. Zody cried out in pain.

"If I fail," continued Arik, "I shall have you to use as—shall we say—collateral?"

"Stop!" Jerrid Zwelger pushed his way through the Mardoks toward Zody and examined his wound. "Why did you do this?" he asked angrily. "You said if I gave you Marcus, you would leave the rest of us alone."

"Did I?" Arik raised an incredulous eyebrow.

Zody, blood trickling down his throat, looked at Jerrid with an expression of disbelief. "*You* betrayed Marcus?" he asked.

"It was for our own good," explained Jerrid. "Marcus lied to us. He knows the truth about Jayson—that Jayson is responsible for Ivanore's disappearance."

Behind them Arik shouted, "Bind them!" The Mardoks obeyed, tying all four boys' hands with ropes.

Jerrid turned his gaze from one boy to the next but was met with lowered eyes. "Jayson is a criminal, don't you see that?!"

Clovis sniffed. "He saved Kelvin's life."

"What do you know, brain-boy? I gave them Marcus to ensure our safety!"

"Maybe Jerrid's right," said Zody, wincing from his wounded chin. "The half-breed might be dangerous, and Marcus—"

"Why do you always side with Jerrid?" said Tristan, turning on Zody with an angry glare. "He treats you worse than a servant and yet you defend him. Jerrid betrayed Marcus because he wanted him out of the way and out of the quest. Why should he share his victory with an orphan?"

The Mardoks dragged Jerrid and the other boys through the square to where freshly saddled horses waited. One Mardok, its hip injured by Kelvin's arrow, limped across the square, joining the others.

On finding Bryn missing, Arik's anger swelled. "Which one of you was guarding the creature?" he shouted.

The injured Mardok stepped forward and knelt before Arik. Arik lifted his sword and in one swift motion plunged it through the Mardok's chest. The Mardok crumpled silently at his feet. Arik and the remaining four Mardoks mounted their horses, a captive boy secured with ropes to the back of each Mardok's saddle.

"We must hurry!" Arik called out. The horses stomped their hooves in the dust. "To Dokur!"

Then, like a crash of thunder, his horse bolted forward with the Mardoks' horses in close pursuit.

Twenty-seven

Several miles outside of Noam the wagon settled into a steady pace, with Kelvin seated on the bench and Marcus in the back. Marcus thought of Tristan, Clovis, and Zody and felt a pang of guilt for having left them behind. He hoped they would not hold it against him, but even if they did, things were better this way, for the less they knew of the truth, the safer they would be from the likes of Arik and his brutal Mardoks. As for Jerrid, Marcus could only hope he'd come to his senses. Once he knew the truth about Jayson, surely Jerrid would regret his betrayal and make amends.

To the south of the road on which Marcus and Kelvin now traveled was a thick grove of trees. Ahead of them the sun was setting beyond a flat horizon of green pastures and deep brown earth. Marcus had never before seen the sun descend beyond anything other than the Jeweled Mountains, and he was awed by its splendor.

After some time had passed, he called up to Kelvin. "Do you think we've separated ourselves enough from Arik? Maybe we should camp in those trees. We could light a fire, trap a little supper."

Kelvin held the reins tightly in his hands. "Arik might approach us by night," he said. "We will have to find a place out of sight to camp."

"But there's almost no shelter out here. How can we hide the wagon and the horses?" asked Marcus.

"We'll have to send them back to the village. They're not ours to keep, anyway. And Dokur can't be more than two or three days' walk from here. We can conceal our tracks better on foot."

They continued on for half an hour more until they reached a bend in the road where it followed the curve of a small stream. Farther north, the stream wound through tall bulrushes and into a grove of willow trees.

"We'll camp here," said Kelvin. He stepped down from the wagon and helped Marcus out as well. Then, taking the horses' reins, he guided them around until they were facing back toward Noam. "All right, I hope you girls know the way home."

Suddenly there was a shriek, and the pile of blankets in the wagon bed flew about in every direction. A young boy with tousled hair jumped out of the wagon with a squeal, as though someone had lit his feet on fire.

"Bryn!" shouted Marcus, trying to regain his composure from the fright. "Bryn, what are you doing here?"

Bryn appeared to be just as frightened as Marcus and Kelvin. He gasped for breath. "Don't send me back!" he pleaded. "I was hiding in the wagon when you seized it and rode it out of town like madmen! I didn't mind that, of course, since getting as far away from those Mardoks as possible sounded like a good plan to me. But now that you're sending the horses back—"

Kelvin quickly readied his bow and leveled an arrow between Bryn's eyes. "You aren't wanted here," he said. "Marcus, get behind me!"

Marcus hesitated.

Kelvin held his aim. Bryn quivered in fear.

"What's wrong with you, Marcus?" Kelvin shouted angrily. "I said get behind me! This monster nearly had me for breakfast yesterday!"

"Please, have mercy!" cried Bryn. "I won't eat you! I swear it!"

"You're a liar!"

"No, it's true! You—" Bryn said, taking a step toward Marcus. Marcus backed away. "Tell him I won't harm you. I owe you my life."

"What is it talking about?" asked Kelvin.

"I helped him escape from Arik," answered Marcus, feeling sheepish.

Kelvin turned on Marcus now but kept his arrow pointed at Bryn.

"You helped it escape?"

"Arik was going to kill him, Kelvin. What else could I do?"

"You could have killed it yourself! That's what I would have done, and it would have been better than it deserved."

The horses whinnied impatiently. Marcus reached up and stroked one of them. He had to admit Kelvin was right. When he had let the Groc go free, he thought he was doing the right thing. But now he wondered if, by doing so, he had put both himself and Kelvin in more danger.

Marcus looked at Bryn and saw the desperation and fear in his eyes. He recalled how quickly Bryn had run from Jayson in the canyon and how helpless he had seemed with Arik. Could it be that he was not such a monster after all?

"I think we should let Bryn come with us," said Marcus.

Kelvin gawked at Marcus as though in shock. "What?"

Marcus continued, justifying his statement before doubt set in. "He won't hurt us, but we'll be on our guard in case he tries. Besides, he could be useful to us."

"That's right," Bryn agreed eagerly, his eyes lighting up with childlike enthusiasm. "Let me live, and I'll protect you in your travels. I can be quite scary. Really!"

Marcus waited for some reaction from Kelvin, but Kelvin only tightened his jaw and remained silent. Marcus turned to Bryn. "Why don't you go gather some wood for a fire? We'll catch some fish for supper."

Bryn nodded, but before he left, he flung his arms around Marcus's waist and hugged him. Then he scampered into the trees like the little boy he was at that moment.

"I don't like this," Kelvin told Marcus once Bryn had gone. "How can you be sure that thing won't kill us both when our backs are turned?"

"Like he said," said Marcus, "he owes me his life."

"You seem awfully sure of his loyalty," replied Kelvin, finally lowering his bow. "I wish I could be as certain of yours."

Twenty-eight

Marcus laid out the wood Bryn had gathered in a small clearing in the trees. As he reached into his satchel for the key, Xerxes spoke up. "It is time for another lesson," he said. "Ready your key. You will try your hand at fire."

"I tried that before and failed," said Marcus quietly so Bryn and Kelvin would not hear him.

"Remember the snake! That surge of flame was no accident. Nor was the fire you created to ward off the Groc. You were frightened then; your emotions were strong. Perhaps your emotions affect the magic."

Marcus examined the key just as he had dozens of times over the past two days. Could Xerxes be right?

Marcus stood at what he hoped was a safe distance from the fire. He held up the key. It felt cold in his hand. He began to feel discouraged but chased the feeling away. I've got to think of something that will create a strong emotion, he thought, but not too strong.

Marcus closed his eyes and tried to remember the day when he was a small boy and he had asked his master why he didn't have a mother and a father. "All the other boys have parents," he had said, his childish face full of expectation. "Why am I different?"

Zyll was younger then but still old in the eyes of a child. He turned away from Marcus and churned the embers in his fireplace with an iron poker. Marcus wondered if he had heard him at all and was about to repeat his question when at last Zyll spoke.

"Your mother died giving birth to you," he said, but this much Marcus had already guessed.

"Did you know her?" he pressed.

Zyll nodded. "Yes, I knew her. She was a woman of great beauty and integrity."

Zyll hung a kettle over the fire to warm. Marcus felt the heat emanate from the cast iron. It felt good radiating against his skin as he tried to imagine his mother's face.

"What about my father?"

Zyll blinked his eyes, and for just a moment his gaze wandered as if his mind had traveled elsewhere. Then, just as quickly, his eyes regained their focus, and his eyebrows knit together. "Supper will be ready soon. Go finish your chores, boy."

"But my father—"

Zyll stood, his demeanor turned brusque. This was not a side to Zyll that Marcus had yet seen, and it frightened him. "You have no father!" Zyll shouted.

Marcus shrank from his master in fear. His young body trembled. Zyll seemed to regret his response the very moment he uttered it. His countenance drooped in sorrow. "Go now," Zyll said softly, "to your chores."

The key in Marcus's hand grew warm. His palm began to sweat. He felt himself trembling. He held the key forward, his arm straight. "Ignite!" he commanded.

Before his lips had finished forming the word, the pile of wood leapt to life, a wild orange flame bursting from it like an angry volcano. The blast was so powerful that the sudden force of it threw Marcus onto his back. Propping himself up on his elbows, he gawked open-mouthed at his creation. The explosion had subsided, leaving behind a manageable fire.

"Did I do that?" Marcus asked, dumbfounded. Bryn, who stared wide-eyed at the blaze, nodded silently. Kelvin glanced up briefly and then went back to setting out his blanket for the night.

Marcus expected praise from Xerxes, but true to his temperament, Xerxes could only find fault. "You're lucky you didn't burn down the whole grove. Where would we have found shelter then?" he scoffed.

Marcus's face reddened. He wanted to take the walking stick and break it over his knee. But instead he turned and stole away silently into the trees.

Twenty-nine

From where he stood just beyond the edge of the glade, Marcus listened to the crackle of the fire. The chill in the night air ran a cold finger down his spine, and he shivered. He tipped his face up toward the heavens and studied the stars. Zyll had taught him how to find the North Star and to use it like a compass. Marcus had always been fascinated by what he read about stars in Zyll's books. When he was alone, he often spent hours creating imaginary pictures by connecting the stars together with invisible lines. Just then a star shot across the horizon, leaving a white trail that faded like a morning mist, and he imagined a horse galloping away.

"Magnificent, isn't it?" Kelvin's voice startled him.

Marcus shivered again. "You're cold. Why not come back to the fire?"

"I want to be alone," Marcus muttered.

"You know," said Kelvin, "when I was little, Mr. Archer would take me into the forest late at night to hunt. Sometimes we'd lie in the same patch of brush for hours. I'd pass the time by counting stars."

Marcus rubbed his arms with his hands for warmth. "I never knew my father," he said.

"The truth is," said Kelvin, "I don't have one either—not really. The Archers took me in when I was very small. I don't remember much about my real parents."

By this time, the moon had risen and hung just above the horizon.

"Why did you come with me?" asked Marcus, changing the subject. "You would have been better off staying with the others."

"I'm drawn to adventure, I suppose," replied Kelvin, pulling his collar up around his chin.

"Really," said Marcus doubtfully.

"That, and I want to know the truth about Jayson. Arik is after him for a reason. What is it, Marcus?"

"Like I said before, I can't tell you anything."

"I understand. It's true I was angry at first, but I've been thinking about what you said. I guess if I had a secret to tell, I'm glad to know I could trust you with it." Kelvin took a deep breath of the cool night air and expelled it in a pale cloud.

Marcus thought of the pendant that hung around his neck. In the excitement and confusion of their escape, he had forgotten about it. Though he had taken it out of anger, he never intended to keep it. Now, after hearing Kelvin's words, he felt ashamed. He wanted to return the pendant, but the moment seemed awkward.

"It's chilly over here," said Kelvin. "You should come sit by the fire." Then he walked away, leaving Marcus alone. The moment for truth passed.

Thirty

The air grew colder with each passing minute. Marcus had just decided to return to the campfire when a twig snapped behind him. Before he could react, someone clamped a hand around his mouth. Fear shot through him like an arrow. A voice whispered in his ear. "Why are you following me?"

The voice was familiar. The hand around his mouth loosened its grip. Marcus turned to face his captor.

"Jayson! How did you—"

"What are you doing out here?" demanded Jayson.

"I came to warn you," answered Marcus, rubbing the pain from his cheeks where Jayson had gripped too tightly.

"Warn me?"

"There's a man looking for you."

"Arik." Jayson said the name with obvious disdain.

There was a shout from the direction of the fire. Marcus saw Bryn snatch a piece of roasted fish from the fire and run off to the safety of a nearby tree.

"You've brought the monster *with* you?" asked Jayson.

"I had no choice!" replied Marcus. "When Arik asked if he recognized me, if I had been with *you*, Bryn protected me. If I hadn't let Bryn come, Arik would have killed him."

"Did Arik follow you?"

"No, I don't think so."

"Of course, why should he?" Jayson said. "He has only one goal in mind, and it isn't chasing a couple of boys through the forest."

"Why is he after you?"

Jayson studied the stars above and then squinted through the trees toward the road. Marcus sensed Jayson's reluctance, but having given his pledge, Marcus felt entitled to some answers.

"The library's history said Ivanore was kidnapped," pressed Marcus. "If I've given my word to a criminal, I have a right to know."

To his surprise, Jayson only smiled. "Yes, I suppose you do have that right," he said, rubbing his temples with his fingers. "I didn't kidnap Ivanore. What I told you before is the truth. She is my wife—and Arik's sister. Arik and I were like brothers. When Fredric exiled me, Arik came to my defense. He even went so far as to draw his sword against his own father. For that, he was disowned and exiled along with me."

Marcus's head swam with this new information. He didn't even notice the cold anymore.

"If you were friends, why does he want to kill you now?"

"Over the past fifteen years," answered Jayson, "Arik has been plotting revenge: overthrowing his father's throne and taking over the realm. Despite what Arik and Ivanore's father did to me, I cannot allow Arik to succeed. Too many innocent lives are at stake. I just hope I reach Dokur before it's too late."

A cool breeze rustled the leaves underfoot and Marcus shivered.

"You should get some rest," continued Jayson. "We've a long journey ahead of us."

"We? You mean you want us to go with you?" Marcus was both excited and apprehensive at the same time. He glanced back at Kelvin, who was shouting obscenities at Bryn. "All of us?"

"Unless you've better things to do."

"But it's dangerous," said Marcus. "You said yourself you might be arrested—or killed!"

"True," replied Jayson, turning his gaze up to the stars. "But some things are worth dying for."

Marcus considered this a moment. Jayson was obviously the reckless type, and traveling with him to Dokur could prove perilous. Marcus had spent his entire life being cautious, doing what was expected of him, what was safe. But now, sitting here listening to Jayson, Marcus felt a peculiar desire—no, *need*—to take a risk.

"I'm coming with you," he said with more certainty

than he thought himself capable. "We'll all come."

A bit of mist escaped Jayson's mouth as he breathed. "It's settled then," he added with a sudden cheerfulness. He held out a rabbit hanging from his fist. "I had planned a feast for one. I'm sure it will be enough to share. A few hours of sleep, and we'll be off."

Jayson patted Marcus on the shoulder, then headed toward the fire.

On one hand, Marcus was pleased that Jayson had asked him to come along. But deep inside, he was filled with a gnawing dread.

Thirty-one

Arik and the Mardoks rode straight through the night, stopping only once to allow the horses to drink from the river and then continuing on. Tristan, Clovis, and Zody managed to sleep occasionally, but sleep would not come to Jerrid. Being tied upright on the back of a horse was uncomfortable at best, and he preferred to wait until he was allowed a proper bed. At one point during the night, he could have sworn he saw a flicker of light through the trees to their left. Though he was certain Arik had seen it, too, their pace remained steady.

Shortly before sunrise, they came upon a lake. The opposite shore was cloaked in a light mist illuminated by the receding moonlight. Arik ordered the Mardoks to lead the horses to the water, but as they neared, the horses began to grunt and stomp the ground.

"They're frightened," said one of the Mardoks. "Something's out there."

"Nonsense!" replied Arik. "Bring me the second bird, and be quick!"

The Mardok dismounted, leaving Jerrid alone atop the horse. From a crate, he retrieved a bird with an orange band about its leg.

"Why the birds?" asked Jerrid. "Who are you trying to contact?"

Arik glanced up at the insolent boy for only a moment. "My business is not your concern," he said.

"Then why the rush to beat Jayson to Dokur?"

Zody shifted nervously on the back of his horse. "Jerrid, what are you doing?!" he said in a forced whisper.

"I saw the campfire back there, same as you. It must have been Jayson," Jerrid continued. "You could have killed him if you really wanted."

Arik's lips grew thin and pale as he pressed them together. He could have bored a hole right through Jerrid with his eyes. But the loathing in his face disappeared as quickly as it came. He took the bird from the Mardok and checked its band.

"I haven't time for distractions now," he said. "Our swift arrival at the northwest harbor is expected."

"What will happen to us when you get there?"

Arik flicked his reins and maneuvered his horse until it was within inches of Jerrid's. He now wore an excessively patient expression, as if he had all the time in the world to spare.

"My contact within the Fortress of Dokur awaits my final signal: a red-banded bird signifying that the tower is secured and the invasion has begun. *If* I fail in my mission and my betrayal is discovered, I will ransom your pathetic lives in exchange for my own. If I succeed . . ." continued Arik, the corners of his lips curling upward ever so slightly, "if I succeed, I will take pleasure in killing you."

Arik released the bird with the orange band. The sound of its wings in the still night air startled the already restless horses. Then another sound rolled across the lake, a low rumble, as if something large and heavy were being dragged along the ground.

"Did you hear that?" whispered Tristan, who sat on the horse beside Jerrid's.

Clovis nodded, biting his lip to keep from crying out in fear. Zody sat on his horse, stiff as a statue. All their eyes were focused on the lake. Though the thickening mist prevented them from clearly seeing the other side, Tristan was sure he saw movement in the shadows.

"We're going to be eaten alive!" whimpered Clovis.

"Shhh!" said Tristan.

A shadow rose up over the far shore, reaching skyward until it blocked the moon from view. Clovis fainted, but as he was tied to his horse, he remained where he sat. Jerrid's horse, however, reared up. The ropes gave way, and Jerrid fell to the ground with a thud.

"Jerrid!" Zody called to him. "Help me out of these

ropes! I want to come with you!" Zody's Mardok host struck him with the back of his hand while the others tried to calm their horses. In the confusion, Jerrid wasted no time in getting to his feet and darting away into the nearest thicket.

Zody watched Jerrid's retreat, his lip already swelling from the Mardok's blow. "Did you see that?" he said to Tristan and Clovis, his voice a choked whisper. "He left me behind."

The Mardok on the ground quickly mounted his horse, making ready to follow his escaped prisoner.

"Let him go!" shouted Arik. "We haven't time to search for him. And besides," he continued, motioning for the others to follow him as he urged his horse onward, "whatever is out there will save us the trouble."

Thirty-two

It was dark when Marcus awoke to the smell of damp ash, the remains of the previous night's fire. A thin film of moisture covered his face. He stood up and peered through the haze. The darkness around him was not the darkness of nighttime, but of a heavy mist that hung in the air like an ethereal phantom. He held his hand up in front of his face but saw nothing.

"Jayson?" His voice echoed back, hollow and empty. "Kelvin? Bryn!"

The fog swirled around him, suffocating him. He held out his hands and took a step forward, but then a terrifying thought struck him: I'm alone!

As the darkness pressed in on him, he fought the urge

to run, for he knew that if he wandered blindly in the dark, he might become lost.

For a moment, panic set in, but then he remembered that he was not completely alone after all. He felt along the ground until his fingers found the walking stick. "Xerxes, wake up!" he said. The eagle squawked loudly.

"I was having a lovely dream until you so rudely . . . Oh my!" Xerxes shivered in Marcus's hands. Marcus was glad to have someone to talk to until he could locate the others.

"Xerxes, it seems that—"

"I'm blind!" shouted Xerxes. "My eyes have been put out! Everything has gone dark!" He was hysterical, and Marcus was afraid he might cry.

"You're not blind," said Marcus. "There's a mist this morning, that's all." In trying to comfort Xerxes, he felt comforted himself, though he could not shake his increasing apprehension. Determined to remain calm, he called out again. "Jayson! Kelvin!"

"Here!" Kelvin's voice cut through the dense vapor like a beam of light.

Marcus felt the comforting warmth of another person's presence. Kelvin grasped his arm.

"You all right?" Kelvin asked.

"I am now," answered Marcus. "This fog . . . I've never seen anything like it. Where are Jayson and Bryn?"

"Here," said Jayson's voice beside him. "Since we can't see well enough to navigate by land, I think it would be best to follow the river downstream."

Kelvin let go of Marcus, and immediately the dark seemed to close in on him again.

"Wait!" Marcus said, the familiar anxiety returning. "I'm all turned around."

Bryn's small child's hand slipped into his.

"The fog doesn't bother me," said Bryn, calling out to Jayson and Kelvin, as well. "Grocs use our sense of smell to travel at night. I can lead you."

Kelvin grasped Marcus's other hand and placed a rope in his palm. "Hold onto this," he said, ignoring Bryn. "It's the only way to stay together."

"That's all right, Bryn," said Jayson. "We Agorans get around pretty well at night, too."

Jayson led Marcus and Kelvin down a gently sloping hill. The ground beneath their feet became soft and soggy, and soon they were standing in six inches of rapidly moving water.

"Wouldn't it be safer to wait until the fog lifts?" asked Marcus.

"We haven't any time to waste. And besides," said Jayson, "this isn't fog. Well, not really."

"If it isn't fog, what is it?" Marcus felt the rope grow taut in his hand. Kelvin, who walked ahead of him, pulled him gently along as they followed Jayson downstream.

"It's laundry day," said Jayson.

"Laundry day?" repeated Marcus. "What's laundry day?"

Thirty-three

"What do you mean 'laundry day'?" Kelvin sounded as perplexed as Marcus felt.

"You'll understand what I mean when we reach Lake Olsnar," said Jayson. "It's not far. This stream will lead us right to it."

They followed the stream for another quarter of an hour. By the time they reached the lake, the mist was so concentrated that it saturated their clothes with water. Marcus felt as though he had waded through the lake itself. Jayson led them around the lake and up a hill. The mist grew thinner until, at the top of the hill, the air was clear. The sun shone brightly overhead, but the valley below was a soft, cottony blanket of vapor.

Jayson pointed to the opposite side of the lake. "Look there," he said.

Marcus strained his eyes to see through the swirls of white, and then he saw it, or rather, he saw *them*. At least a dozen heads and shoulders seemed to float above the mist like massive marble sculptures. On closer inspection, however, Marcus realized that the heads were not floating at all. They were attached to entire bodies—bodies so tall that their upper halves rose above the surface of the fog. The giants moved methodically through the vapor, which spilled over the rims of several massive black vats.

"Who are they?" asked Kelvin. Marcus was too astounded to speak. He had never seen a giant before.

"Cyclopes," said Jayson. Marcus looked again, and though he hadn't realized it at first, he now saw that each giant's face had only one large eye in the center of its forehead. Kelvin strung his bow and leveled an arrow toward the lake, but Jayson took the arrow in his fist. "They're harmless," he said.

"Harmless?" said Kelvin. "They've killed humans before!"

"Only in self-defense," Jayson explained. "Cyclopes may be big, but they are gentle creatures."

The Cyclopes stirred their vats with large wooden paddles. One lifted a steaming giant-sized article of clothing from a vat and hung it on the branch of a nearby tree.

Laundry day.

Jayson stood and, cupping his hands around his mouth, called out. "Hello there! Hello!"

He waved his arms in the air. The Cyclopes stopped stirring to look up. When they saw Jayson, they began to talk animatedly among themselves. One Cyclops came forward, walking through the lake as if it were nothing more than a shallow swamp. When it reached the other side, it knelt down and rested its chin on top of the hill.

"*Wiloth*, Jayson," it said in a voice that was both melodious and breathy. "*Eebreth undraja beyosh?*"

Jayson smiled warmly at the gentle giant and rubbed the side of its bald head with his hand. "*Eetu*," he said. "*Yalay anoreth Dukar.*"

Bryn tugged on Marcus's sleeve. "What did it say?" he whispered.

"He's welcoming Jayson back," said Marcus, surprised at how easily the translation came. "It speaks a dialect of the ancient tongue."

Bryn cowered behind him, frightened by the sheer size of the Cyclopes. Jayson rubbed behind the Cyclops's ears. The creature closed its eye and purred like a kitten.

"I take it they're friends of yours?" Kelvin asked Jayson.

"Yes. This one's name is Breah."

"I didn't think there were any of them left on this part of the island."

"Like the Agorans, the Cyclopes have been forcibly removed from their lands," explained Jayson. "Only a few bands of them remain in this valley, but it's only a matter of time before they'll be forced out, as well."

Jayson continued speaking with the Cyclops in its own tongue. Marcus recognized many of the words. A second

Cyclops soon appeared through the mist. Its greeting surprised Marcus, for it spoke not in the ancient tongue, but in the language of humans.

"I thought I heard a familiar voice," it said. This Cyclops's hair was speckled with gray and there was only a scar where its eye should have been. "The others believed you had passed to the next life, but I knew one day Jayson would again be in our midst."

"*Wiloth*, Vos," said Jayson respectfully.

"Will you stay and feast with us?" asked Vos.

"I'm sorry, but no," replied Jayson. "My time is short. I must reach Dokur by midday tomorrow."

"Dokur? There is nothing there but thieves and vandals. Better to stay here among friends."

"I must go," said Jayson, giving Breah one last rub behind the ears. Vos raised his one bushy eyebrow.

"You go to find Ivanore. I know what they say about her, that she is lost," said Vos, "but do not be so quick to believe what you hear. Many believed you were lost, and yet here you stand."

"Ivanore lost? I don't understand."

"I know little except what I hear in the breeze. Perhaps you will learn more when you reach your destination. Is there anything I can do to be of assistance?"

Jayson nodded. "One thing. We are being followed by a group of Mardoks. Could you detain them should they come by the lake?"

Vos scratched his gray head with a long, bony finger. "A group of horsemen passed by this morning before daybreak. But they have long since gone their way. I am sorry."

"It is of no consequence, my friend," said Jayson. "Do not concern yourself. I must be on my way now. Perhaps the gods will allow our paths to cross again one day."

Jayson said his goodbyes, and the Cyclopes returned to their laundry. As Marcus followed Jayson down the opposite side of the hill, he hesitated to ask any more about their brief encounter with the Cyclopes, but what Vos said concerned him.

"The horsemen Vos spoke of, could they be the Mardoks?"

"Yes," answered Jayson. "Arik must have passed us during the night. We haven't much time."

Thirty-four

As Marcus and the others reached the bottom of the hill at the far side of Lake Olsnar, the mist grew dense once again. Without the river nearby, Marcus feared that navigating would be impossible.

"We'll never find our way through this," said Kelvin, handing Marcus the rope. "Why don't you use that key of yours?"

Bryn was already digging in Marcus's pocket for it. He fished it out and held it up like a trophy. "Shiny!" he said.

Marcus took it from Bryn and rubbed it clean on his cape. "How can you tell what it looks like in *this*?" Marcus asked, indicating the cloud in which they were standing.

"Grocs can see even better than we smell," replied Bryn proudly.

"I can believe that," Kelvin retorted. "Do Grocs *ever* take baths?"

Marcus rubbed the key between his palms and tried to decide the best plan of action. He wished he could speak to Xerxes, but with Kelvin and Jayson near, that was not an option. As though he could read Marcus's thoughts, Xerxes' eyes fluttered open.

"I couldn't help but overhear your conversation," he said with a wide yawn. "I know you cannot speak, so just listen. Squeeze the staff if you understand."

Marcus gave one long squeeze with his hand.

"Not too tight. I'm not made of iron, you know! So how should we deal with this fog? You could condense the vapor into water, but that much water would turn the ground beneath us into a swamp." Xerxes clicked his beak rapidly, and Marcus imagined the look of concentration that must be on his wooden face. "You might heat the mist so that it would rise. No, no. Where could you harvest enough energy to warm that much water? I will have to think . . ."

Marcus decided to do what would take as little effort as possible. He held the key in front of him and focused his attention. He was about to utter a single command, but thought better of it. Remembering the snake in the forest, he chose instead to try giving his command in silence. I must choose wisely, he cautioned himself, or it might backfire and end up causing a hurricane or something.

He settled on the word *divide* and repeated it in his mind. The key heated up more quickly than he expected.

The mist began to churn like a small cyclone, which split into two halves, each spinning in opposite directions. The fog parted before him as though invisible hands had reached down and split a bale of cotton in two.

Marcus tested the nearest patch of mist with the tip of the walking stick. It had not changed its composition but curled about the staff like angels' breath.

"Not what I would have done," said Xerxes, "but effective nonetheless."

Marcus grinned with pleasure at Xerxes' half-hearted compliment. Then, pocketing the key, he led Kelvin and Jayson along the straight, clear path until, several hours later, the fog finally lifted.

They continued walking in silence, the hours passing slower than Marcus ever thought possible. Ahead of him, Kelvin followed Bryn, who trudged wearily several paces behind Jayson.

"I'm hungry," said Bryn finally. "When are we going to stop?"

Using his crossbow, Kelvin prodded Bryn from behind. "Keep walking," he said.

"Didn't you hear him?" said Marcus. "He said he's hungry."

"We're all hungry," replied Kelvin, giving Bryn another nudge. "The only difference is we humans don't eat each other."

Bryn stopped suddenly and turned toward Kelvin. "I told you before—I won't eat you."

"And what if I don't believe you?" said Kelvin. "All we

have to do is close our eyes for a second, and you'll turn into that monster thing and we're through."

Bryn did not reply. Instead he bit his bottom lip to keep it from trembling. Tears pooled in his eyes. "You hate me," he said, "don't you?"

"Of course I hate you! You tried to chew me up and swallow me for lunch!"

At this point Marcus thought it best to intervene. He placed his arm around Bryn's shoulders and urged him gently forward. The three of them began walking again.

"And why does a Groc travel with humans, anyway?" asked Kelvin. "Don't you have a herd or brood of other Grocs to go home to? Won't they miss you?"

Bryn glanced down at his feet as they walked. He was quiet for several moments before speaking. "No one misses me," he said. "And I do not miss them. I left because I do not want to be a Groc anymore. I want to be—" Bryn hesitated. He looked up at Marcus, who gave him a reassuring smile. Then Bryn spoke again. "I want to be human."

Kelvin burst out laughing. "A Groc wants to be human! Did you hear that, Jayson?"

Jayson, who was now several yards ahead of the others, called back. "I heard him."

"If you want to be human," continued Kelvin, "why did you attack us in the canyon?"

"I was so hungry," answered Bryn defensively. "I try not to be a . . . a monster . . . but sometimes I cannot help it."

The road on which they traveled grew steeper. Soon it bent through a densely wooded area. Marcus heard the sound of bubbling water nearby and hoped they would stop there to rest.

"If you cannot help being who you are," continued Kelvin, "how can you expect us to trust you?"

Bryn stopped walking once again and looked directly into Kelvin's eyes. His expression was solemn. "Because," he said in as serious a tone as Marcus had heard him use, "I promise. And unlike most humans, I keep my promises."

Thirty-five

The day grew unusually warm, and Marcus wiped away another trickle of sweat from his forehead. He gazed at his reflection in the spring from which he had just filled his water skin. The surface was in constant motion, making the image of his face distort in humorous ways, and he laughed at himself.

"Are the fish telling jokes now?" asked Jayson, sidling up beside him and dropping to his knees in the soft mud. He cupped his hands and dipped them in the cold water, drinking from them repeatedly. When he had finished, he sat down on a flat boulder and stretched out his legs. "After lunch we'll continue. We should reach Dokur by midday tomorrow," he said, scratching the stubble on his chin.

Marcus was glad the journey would not be long. On the eastern side of the Jeweled Mountains, the weather was cold, and frost would soon be garnishing the fields each morning. Yet here in the open valleys of the west, the air was near sweltering. A weak breeze and the cool water of the spring were their only relief.

"Are there many villages along the way?" asked Marcus.

"There used to be, but most moved out long ago," Jayson explained. "Like the Cyclopes, my people once inhabited this entire valley, but when the humans migrated here from the mainland, things changed."

"But you're part human . . ." Marcus let his voice drift off, afraid he might offend his companion.

Yet Jayson appeared to take no offense. "Yes, my father is human. By the time I was born, the Agoran tribes had been removed to a reservation in Taktani, a piece of marshland fit only for frogs and flies. My mother died there. Things got so bad that eventually they sent me to petition Lord Fredric for aid. Because I was half human, they thought he might listen to me. They were wrong."

Marcus watched Jayson, waiting for more.

Jayson sensed his interest and continued. "That's when I met her."

"Ivanore?"

Jayson smiled at her memory. "She was the most beautiful thing I had ever seen. Long silky hair the color of autumn wheat. Eyes as blue as the sky. And her skin . . ." Jayson held up his hand and stroked an invisible cheek with his fingers. Then he dropped his hand on the rock beside him, becoming melancholic. "It was a long time ago," he finished.

Marcus dug his toe into the mud. He sensed Jayson's reluctance to go on with his story, but it intrigued him so that he dared to press him further. "You said your mother died. What about your father? Is he still in Taktani?"

Jayson's countenance hardened. "I haven't seen my father since I was a boy. The Agorans do not trust humans and vice versa. My parents were forced to separate. Ivanore was taken from me—all because we are different from each other."

Marcus thought of the isolation he often felt because of being different. While the other boys learned the art of hunting from their fathers, Marcus spent his time with books. How he had longed to join in their games, and at times he had resented his station. But as he grew older, he came to accept who he was—though feelings of resentment still surfaced now and then.

Jayson slapped his hand into the water, upsetting the reflection there. As he rose to his feet, a sudden ear-piercing squeal sounded in the distance. Jayson and Marcus looked at each other as though reading one another's thoughts. Both of them scrambled to their feet and took off running.

"Bryn!" shouted Marcus as he neared the grove of trees where they had stopped earlier to rest. "Kelvin! Where are you?"

Marcus and Jayson found Kelvin leaning against a tree, gasping for breath. He held his dagger in his hand.

"What happened?" asked Marcus. "We heard something cry out."

"Bryn," began Kelvin, trying to catch his breath. "He attacked me. I was resting against this tree when I heard a low growl. I opened my eyes and saw him coming toward me, his figure changed into that beast from the canyon. He lunged at me. I hardly had time to think. I swung my dagger blindly at him."

"Where is he?" asked Marcus, but Jayson was already heading deeper into the woods.

Kelvin pointed to a large clump of bushes nearby. "He landed past me in that thicket over there."

Marcus hurried to the spot and arrived just as Jayson began hacking through the shrub. A moment later they found Bryn, a boy once again, lying face down on the earth, half buried in vines and vegetation.

Seeing Bryn's still form, Marcus wondered what had prompted Bryn to break his promise. He had been so certain that Bryn would not harm them. How could he have so misjudged the Groc's character?

Kelvin stepped up beside Marcus and placed a hand on his shoulder. "I told you he couldn't be trusted."

Jayson grasped Bryn's arm and carefully rolled him onto his back. Beneath him, a young warboar, nearly as big as Bryn, lay dead, a large gaping wound at its neck.

Marcus spoke first. "He . . . Bryn was trying to protect you," he said to Kelvin, a quiver in his voice. "He wasn't attacking you at all."

Jayson poked the warboar with the tip of his sword. "It would have ripped you to shreds with those tusks."

Kelvin stood motionless, staring at Bryn's body. Then he turned and walked away. Marcus wanted to go with him but sensed that Kelvin needed to be alone. Before Kelvin took three steps, however, Bryn moaned.

Kelvin turned back as Marcus dropped to his knees beside Bryn. "You're alive!" said Marcus. "We all thought you were dead. Are you hurt?"

Bryn sat up slowly. "I don't think so," he replied. "I saw a warboar charging toward Kelvin. I threw myself at it but must have smacked my head against a tree. The next thing I know I'm sitting here with you."

Jayson helped Bryn to his feet. "Good," he said, laughing. "You can scout out the next several miles of road while we prepare this warboar for lunch."

Bryn brushed the leaves and twigs from his clothes and rubbed the tender spot on the back of his head. Kelvin stood nearby, a contrite look on his face. "What I said before," he began, "I was wrong about you. I hope you'll forgive me."

"You don't hate me anymore?" asked Bryn.

Kelvin shook his head. "I don't hate you anymore."

Kelvin held out his hand to Bryn, but Bryn did not take it. For a moment Kelvin hesitated, not knowing how to respond should his apology be rejected. But when Bryn stepped forward and embraced him, it was clear that Kelvin had been forgiven.

Thirty-six

Jerrid Zwelger spent the better part of the day crouching beneath a bush far off the main road. The mist that had rolled across the lake provided the cover he needed to escape from the Mardoks, but when the air cleared, he had to settle for the cramped hiding space embedded with thorns. He stayed there for as long as he could bear. But finally, at the urging of his empty stomach, he ventured out.

The ground felt marshy beneath his feet. The willows growing along the lakeshore swayed in the breeze. He caught a whiff of baking bread and followed it around the lake to a cluster of Willenberry trees. A thin tendril of smoke curled up from the treetops, and Jerrid went toward it, hoping to find a hospitable host and a warm meal.

After several minutes, he came upon a grassy clearing. In the center stood a massive structure made of stone. As he drew nearer, he saw that it was an oven, an oven taller than his home in Quendel. The oven's door alone was more than twice as tall as he was. What or who would need an oven of such proportions did not cross his mind; the sweet fragrance of bread wafting out of it was all he cared about.

It wasn't until the Cyclops had him in his grip that he began to scream. Jerrid screamed so long and so loudly that he only stopped to suck in enough air to continue screaming. The Cyclops held him at eye level and cocked his head to one side. Certain the monster was about to take a bite out of him, Jerrid's screams turned to tearful wails. The cacophony brought other Cyclopes in from the trees, and soon more than a dozen of them encircled Jerrid, still in the clutches of his one-eyed captor.

Jerrid's wails turned to sobs and then to intermittent sniffs and whimpers. When he realized that he was not going to be eaten, his crying stopped altogether. "W-why haven't you k-killed me?" he asked, wiping the tears from his face with his sleeve. "Aren't you hungry?"

The Cyclops that held him looked bewildered. "*Urtur ah Breah,*" he said.

Jerrid tried again. "I thought you would have eaten me by now. You know . . . eat." He lifted his fingers to his mouth as though he were putting food into it.

The Cyclops repeated the same phrase as before, copying Jerrid's gesture. "*Urtur ah Breah.*"

"No," said Jerrid. He was beginning to feel frustrated. If the monsters were going to eat him, he would prefer to get it over with quickly. "If you're not going to have me for supper, let me go!" he shouted.

The crowd of Cyclopes shifted, and an elderly one came forward. He was bent with years, and a wide jagged scar marred his forehead.

"Who is there?" the blind Cyclops said.

He speaks my language! Jerrid realized, relieved to know that someone would be able to understand him.

"My name is Jerrid," he said. "I was hungry and smelled the bread cooking in your oven. I didn't know what . . . that *you* lived here, or I wouldn't have come."

The Cyclops that held him spoke again. "*Urtur ah Breah.*"

"He says his name is Breah," explained the old Cyclops. "I am Vos. By your voice I sense you are but a child. What is a boy doing alone at Lake Olsnar?"

"I'm fourteen, actually," said Jerrid. "I'm on a quest."

Vos spoke to Breah in the Cyclopes' language, and Breah set Jerrid gently on the ground.

"You smell familiar," said Vos. "I've smelled you before, but it was many years ago, before your time."

Jerrid remembered the stories of his father, how he had carried home a Cyclops's eye for his prize. He decided he should change the subject—and fast.

"That bread smells delicious," he said. "May I trouble you for some?"

Vos requested that Jerrid be fed. He was not only

given bread, but also roasted yams, cabbage salad, and nectar, as well. By the time he had finished eating, Jerrid was glad he had stumbled upon the Cyclopes.

"I should be going," he said after thanking them for his meal. "I have to get to Dokur."

When Vos heard the word *Dokur*, he dropped his massive hand on the ground in front of Jerrid.

"Why do you go to Dokur?" he asked.

"I told you before," replied Jerrid. "I'm on a quest."

"What is the nature of your quest?"

Jerrid hesitated. But then he thought, what would Cyclops care about Jayson?

"I seek the Rock of Ivanore," he said.

Vos and the other Cyclopes gasped. They began speaking with one another in frenzied voices. Vos held up his hand to silence them. He leaned over and sniffed the air above Jerrid. Then he opened his mouth and roared. The sound was deafening.

"I know that stench now!" Vos bellowed angrily. "It is the smell of the creature that blinded me and left me for dead more than twenty-five years ago!"

"No!" shouted Jerrid, suddenly terrified. "It wasn't me!"

"It could not have been you, but your smell is the same as his. How can that be?"

"It w-was m-my father!" Jerrid's legs turned to jelly. He struggled to remain standing.

"And now you, O spawn of my enemy," continued Vos, "you want to go to Dokur to destroy the only friend the Cyclopes have on all of Imaness! He who taught me to speak his language! He who defended us against the invasion of humans! You will not harm him!"

Jerrid found himself once again in Breah's grasp, but this time there was loathing in the Cyclops's face. With his free hand, Breah opened the great door to the stone oven and tossed Jerrid inside. Then he slammed the door shut with a bang.

Jerrid looked around him. A narrow shaft of light filtered in through the chimney above. The chimney was wide enough for him to escape, but its opening was too high for him to reach. The walls of the oven were still warm, and Jerrid feared that they would light a fire underneath it and cook him for supper after all. With nothing else for him to do, he dropped to his knees in the center of the cavernlike space and wept.

Thirty-seven

The sun was high overhead by the time Bryn returned from surveying the road ahead. In the Groc's absence, Jayson had deftly skinned and cleaned the warboar. A large piece of it was now roasting over a generous fire.

"Did you scout the area?" asked Jayson.

Bryn eyed the warboar hungrily. "I want some," he said.

"Not until you give your report."

Bryn scowled. "I never agreed to be your slave," he snapped.

"What did you find out there?"

"Nothing," said Bryn, folding his arms stubbornly across his chest.

Jayson reached out and sliced a chunk from the war-boar and dangled it in front of Bryn. Bryn snatched it and tore off a piece with his pointy teeth.

"Now," said Jayson, "tell me what you found."

Bryn finished his meat and licked his fingertips. "There is a hill not a mile up the road, and not far from that a canyon. But I won't go back there," he said, planting his feet firmly on the ground and pointing his chin toward the sky. "You can't make me."

Jayson turned to Marcus and Kelvin. "Shall we have a look? In the meantime, Bryn, you can gather berries for lunch," he said, taking Marcus's satchel and handing it to Bryn. "Put them in this."

Bryn held up the bag indignantly and pinched his nose with his fingers. "Grocs have a keen sense of smell, and *this* smells bad!"

*　　*　　*

Jayson, Marcus, and Kelvin walked the mile to the hill in silence. They ascended it cautiously. As they neared the top, they crawled the rest of the way and peered over the crest. Below them in a deep canyon, hundreds of creatures unlike Marcus had ever before seen were laboring in what appeared to be some sort of mine. The creatures were shaped like men, with agile arms, legs, a head and torso, but a fine fur covered their bodies, and thick manes of it grew on their heads. Their faces were almost catlike, though more human than cat, and their fingers were short and tipped in sharp claws. Most of the cat-men dug against the canyon walls with heavy picks. Others loaded large chunks of earth into wagons, while still others pulled the wagons to a central pile and unloaded them. Scattered among them were large, muscular human guards bearing leather whips.

"What are they?" asked Marcus.

"Agorans," said Jayson. "It seems his Lordship has recruited my people to mine Celestine."

"Slavery is outlawed in Quendel—and in all the villages east of the Jeweled Mountains," said Kelvin.

"And in Dokur as well, but I see things have changed since I've been away. Come. We should go before we are seen."

Jayson started down the hill, but Marcus called out to him. "We can't leave them like this!"

"Your heroism is honorable, but we can do nothing for them."

"We could fight those guards."

"Yes, and we would die," said Jayson. "What good would that do anyone? You obviously did not see the other guards stationed at the base of the canyon, the ones with broadswords strapped about their waists. If you want to help the Agorans, then we must get to Dokur. If we do not arrive in time, everyone—slave and free—will die."

Kelvin and Jayson crawled back down the hill, keeping low to the ground to avoid being seen. Marcus lingered behind. Directly below him a guard whipped a young Agoran boy. The youth cowered on the ground and cried out in pain with each stroke of the whip. Marcus could hardly bear to watch. Then an idea struck him. So far he had manipulated heat and water. What if he could control solid elements? He took Zyll's key from his pocket and held it against a large boulder at the edge of the canyon.

As he began to think of what word he should utter, Xerxes interrupted him. "What do you think you are doing?" he asked.

Fall? Break free? Tumble down? The words raced through Marcus's mind. "I'm trying to loosen this boulder," he replied.

"Do you mean to drop it on one of those men's heads?" Xerxes' voice was reproachful, like a nagging mother. "Surely you remember Zyll's caution. To use magic in such a way is just inviting trouble."

"It's only a rock," said Marcus. "I managed the fog just fine. I know what I'm doing."

"Do you?" replied Xerxes.

Marcus closed his eyes and concentrated. One word, he told himself. I only need one word. But before he could form one in his mind, the boulder began to tremble beneath his hand. He had expected the key to grow hot like before, but this time he noticed that it wasn't so much the key as his own palm that radiated heat. He didn't have time to think about it, however. Within moments the boulder shook loose and plummeted into the canyon below.

The cries stopped. Marcus looked down and saw the boy gaping wide-eyed at the stone and at the injured guard reeling in pain beside it. The stone had landed nearly on top of him.

Marcus brushed off his hands, pleased with himself. But then he noticed the earth beneath him had begun to shift. Small chunks of dirt broke away, falling into the canyon. There was a loud crack, and the section of the cliff where he stood broke away. He barely had time to jump to safety before it hurtled down into the canyon.

"Well, maybe now you'll listen to my advice," scolded Xerxes. "I intend to tell Zyll about this fiasco!"

Marcus glanced over the still-unsteady ledge, fearful that he may have inadvertently injured a slave. Luckily, after the first boulder landed, the Agorans had cleared the area, but even so, Marcus cursed himself for being so careless.

Thirty-eight

The afternoon air had grown thick and humid, and the slight breeze gave no relief. Jayson and Kelvin walked along the roadside aware that Marcus had chosen to remain behind a while longer. After several minutes, the silence between them felt as unpleasant as the air.

"Our journey is going well, don't you think?" asked Jayson, swatting a gnat away from his face. "Or do you wish I hadn't joined you on this expedition?"

Kelvin shifted his crossbow from his right shoulder to his left and took a drink of water from his water skin. "I am going to Dokur to fulfill my quest," he said, replacing the stopper. "That you have decided to come along is of no consequence to me."

"I *did* save your life, you know."

"For which I am grateful."

"Then why do you dislike me so much?"

Kelvin cast Jayson a sideways glance. The ground beneath his feet was hard and rutted. He tripped once, kicking up a cloud of dust. "I don't dislike you," he said.

"But . . ." coaxed Jayson with a mischievous smile.

"But I do resent the way you've manipulated Marcus into trusting you. I know there's some secret he's keeping from the rest of us. I think it has to do with Ivanore."

Jayson's smile faded. They continued for several minutes without speaking.

When Kelvin spoke again, it was with calm restraint. "Did you kidnap Ivanore?"

"Is that what you believe?" asked Jayson. They were nearing the area where they had left Bryn earlier. The road bent slightly, and as they walked along it, Jayson kept his eyes to the ground.

"It's what most people believe, isn't it," said Kelvin, "that an Agoran half-breed took her hostage against her will?"

Jayson turned and grabbed Kelvin by the front of his shirt.

"*That* is a lie!" he shouted. "I love Ivanore! I always will!" His eyes burned with rage, but Kelvin was not deterred.

"You broke the law. Can you deny it?"

When Jayson's eyes met Kelvin's, the anger within him quickly subsided. Jayson released Kelvin and turned away. "No," he said. "I cannot deny it."

"Then how can you continue using Marcus for your own selfish purposes? How can you, in good conscience, allow him to believe you are his friend and ally?"

Kelvin waited for an answer, but there was none. Instead Jayson's eyes scanned the field beyond the bend, and then his gaze dropped once more to the road. "Something is wrong here," he said. "I can feel it."

Thirty-nine

Marcus eased his way down the hill and walked back the way he had come. By the time he reached the bend in the road he felt exhausted—drained of all energy.

"Are you all right?" Kelvin asked as Marcus approached. "You look pale."

"I'm fine," replied Marcus, sprawling out on the grass beside the road. "Where's Bryn?"

"He's gone. We only found this when we returned." Kelvin handed Marcus his satchel half full with berries.

Marcus forced himself back to his feet. His strength was returning. He cupped his hands around his mouth and called for the Groc. "Bryn! Bryn!" No answer came.

"Maybe he went back into the woods for more berries," he suggested.

Through narrowed eyes, Jayson searched the road and the trees that lined it. "Perhaps," he agreed, though the tone of his voice suggested he did not fully accept that explanation—yet he offered no other.

Marcus picked up a handful of berries and weighed them in his palm. "Should we wait for him to come back?"

Kelvin drew an arrow from his quiver and prepared his bow.

"What are you doing?" asked Marcus, his voice dropping to a whisper. An uneasiness crept over him, and he felt like a gazelle preparing to bolt at the scent of an unseen predator. Standing in the open road with a wide, flat field on one side and a small grove of trees on the other, he longed for the protection of the Jeweled Mountains. He noticed Jayson's hand twitch nervously as it rested against his sword. He drew his own blade from Xerxes' sheath and held it ready in front of him.

The air was nearly still. Only the slightest breeze brushing through the dry grass of the plain broke the silence. Like a sudden explosion, four galloping horses burst through the trees. With not a moment to think, Marcus dove into the high grass behind him as a blur of hooves flew past, missing him by mere inches. He rolled to the right and jumped to his feet. At the same moment, Jayson managed to snag the leg of a passing rider with his claws. The rider hit the ground hard but wasted no time in drawing his sword. He wore thick leather armor on his chest. In his left hand he held a round shield painted red with a yellow cross. Jayson's sword came down on it with a sharp clang. The guard struggled to his feet, and they continued their conflict.

The other three riders were dressed like the first and carried the same patterned shields. One sat in his saddle moaning in pain, an arrow jutting out of his left shoulder. Another had dismounted and now grappled with Kelvin on the ground. Marcus did not wait to see where the fourth rider had gone. He ran toward Kelvin, roaring like a wild animal, and buried the point of his sword between the shoulder blades of the guard. The injured guard screamed and stumbled forward, reaching his hands behind his back in an effort to remove the object embedded there. The second guard snapped off the arrow from his shoulder and also dismounted. Fear swelled inside Marcus. He was now without a weapon, and even if he did have one, he was no match for the muscular brute that stood before him.

Raising his broadsword, the guard bared his teeth in a sinister grimace. Marcus thought to run, but in an instant the guard bolted forward, his sword readied to sever Marcus's head from his body. Just as he took his first step, however, his face contorted. He stopped where he stood, his eyes rolled back in his head, and he fell face first to the ground, an arrow stuck in his back. Kelvin was on his knees in the center of the road, his bow still ready and his chest heaving.

Marcus noticed, too, that the guard that had been fighting with Jayson now lay motionless in the grass. A stream of blood stained Jayson's sleeve.

"Where did those riders come from? Who were they?" asked Marcus.

"Fredric's scouts," replied Jayson.

Marcus jerked his sword from the now-dead guard's back and cleaned it on the grass. "There were four of them."

"The last one escaped," said Jayson. He examined the shallow gash above his right elbow. "He had Bryn with him."

Kelvin rose to his feet, still gasping for breath. "What will happen to him?" he asked.

"All Grocs are felons in Dokur," answered Jayson. "He'll be executed."

Kelvin turned to Marcus, outrage in his face. "What is wrong with you?" he shouted. "Why didn't you use your magic? We were nearly killed! And Bryn's been taken captive!"

"I-I couldn't think. It happened too fast," stammered Marcus. During the conflict the thought of using magic as a defense had never entered his mind. "I'm sorry" were the only words he could think of to say.

"Sorry can't heal wounds," said Kelvin bitterly. "And it won't bring Bryn back!"

His words ended abruptly as his gaze traveled downward to Marcus's chest.

"What is *this*?" he said. Marcus realized too late what Kelvin now saw. Kelvin snatched the pendant in his hand and jerked it free. As the leather cord snapped, a sharp pain shot through Marcus's neck. No more words were said. The betrayed expression on Kelvin's face said it all.

TRUTH REVEALED

Forty

Night again, and Marcus's sleep was shallow and restless. The darkness pressed in on him as before, suffocating him. He struggled against it, tried to push back the memories into the depths where he had kept them for so long. But they returned now against his will.

There was no moon the night Zyll had taken sick. The old man's body had been racked with fever. Marcus was just a boy of eight years, and he feared for his master's life.

Feeling helpless, he asked, "What should I do?"

"Lemonweed," whispered Zyll to Marcus through parched lips. "Go to the herbalist and bring me some."

Marcus took a candle with him and started across the field separating his cottage from the village, but the night was blustery and the candle blew out. It wasn't until he reached the trees that he realized he had gone the wrong way.

Suddenly he heard a sound that made his blood run cold. Only a few yards from where he stood, a warboar grunted and pawed the ground. Marcus turned and ran as fast as his legs would carry him, screaming as loudly as he could for help. When his foot caught on a broken branch, he fell to the ground. In an instant, the warboar was upon him, slashing at him with its sharp tusks. Marcus could still hear the animal's breath against his ears even now.

Just when he was about to give up hope, a light appeared above him. It grew so bright that Marcus had to shield his eyes with his hand. The warboar fled, and Marcus felt the pain within him melt away. I have died, he thought, and this angel has come to take me to heaven.

All of a sudden, he heard shouts of men coming from the village. They had heard Marcus's screams and were coming to his aid. As the light of their torches drew near, the angel's light vanished.

The villagers carried Marcus to the healer, who patched up his injuries and accompanied him back to his master's house. But ever since then, Marcus's sleep had been tormented with nightmares, and he was left with a crippling fear of darkness.

Marcus awoke trembling, his clothes damp with per-spiration. He guessed it was well past midnight by the stars' positions. He glanced at Kelvin and Jayson sleeping nearby and was relieved to know all was well. He was just closing his eyes again when Xerxes startled him.

"You're awake!" said Xerxes, yawning. "Good! We've got work to do!"

"It's too early," Marcus protested.

"Nonsense! Today we learn levitation and transfer—the art of moving solid objects. After the calamity at the mines, you need a little extra training. Now, get up!" he said. "Up! Up! Up!"

Marcus groaned, but instead of obeying, he tossed his cape over Xerxes' head, rolled over, and went back to sleep.

*   *   *

The city of Dokur stood atop the crest of a rocky cliff, its watchtower and the spires of the Fortress jutting skyward like a royal crown. The city's position afforded it absolute protection from those who might wish to attack by land, and the watchtower situated on the shore afforded the guards of Dokur the ability to see so far toward the horizon that no ship could get within ten miles of the island without being detected.

The road to Dokur was steep and narrow, bordered on the left by towering walls of solid granite and on the right by a sheer drop to the valley floor. Marcus crept along while keeping one palm pressed against the rock wall and the other firmly around Xerxes's head. He tested each step as he went, as though he feared the ground beneath him might, at any moment, give way.

"You're slower than a snail!" said Jayson, giving him a gentle shove from behind.

"Don't push me!" Marcus shouted. "Do you want me to fall?"

"You won't fall. If the road is wide enough for wagons, it is certainly wide enough for you."

"Wagons? This trail isn't wide enough for anything other than lizards and rats! One wrong step and that's the end of me."

"How do you suppose they get their supplies? Merchants travel up this road each morning and down again each evening. Wares from all over the island are brought here for trade. And as far as it being the end of you," added Jayson with one more shove, "my stomach is in dire need of food, and should you fall, my hunger might very well take precedence over saving your life."

Marcus went red in the face as Jayson burst into laughter. Even Xerxes laughed at him, but Kelvin's brooding silence quickly brought everyone's laughter to an end.

The sun was high overhead when the road finally leveled off and Dokur spread out before them like a patchwork quilt. Ahead of them lay the urban center of the city where people gathered for trading and other social events. To the east were farms divided into tidy sections by low rock walls. The residential district occupied the central part of Dokur, while the sea lay to the northwest.

The streets of the city, paved with cobblestone, were alive with wagons, horses, and people by the hundreds. The town square was the largest Marcus had ever seen, with a grassy area and an immense marble fountain at its center. Stone buildings two and three stories high towered above them, nearly blocking out the sun. At the top of a nearby hill was the Fortress where Lord Fredric governed the affairs of Dokur Province. Marcus had never in his life seen a place so grand as Dokur, and as they walked through the square, he thought he might never want to leave.

Jayson gazed for a moment at the throngs of people crowding the streets. "Take a close look, boys," he said. "Lord Fredric's idyllic society. No Agorans, no Noamish, no inhumans of any kind."

Jayson led them to a small tavern on the main thoroughfare. The wooden sign that hung above the door read THE SEAFARER TAVERN. "You two wait here," he ordered. "I have to seek an audience with his Lordship. I should be back by nightfall." Jayson started across the street, when Marcus stepped forward, taking him by the arm.

"And if you don't come back?" Marcus asked, wondering if the queasiness he felt was due to hunger or dread.

"Then I suggest you leave Dokur as quickly as you can," Jayson said. Then he added with a wink, "but first, promise me you'll buy yourself a new satchel before you go."

Jayson pulled on his hood and slipped into the crowded marketplace.

Marcus joined Kelvin by the tavern door. "Why doesn't anyone like my satchel?" he asked, but Kelvin made no reply. He tried a different question. "Shall we go inside?" Again Kelvin remained silent. Marcus tried once more. "I said, shouldn't we go in?"

"I heard you," replied Kelvin sharply. The triangular crystal once again hung from his neck, and he rubbed it between his thumb and index finger. Marcus knew Kelvin was angry, and justifiably so. He also knew Kelvin would never forgive him unless he apologized—a situation that would make traveling with him unpleasant, to say the least.

"I'm sorry about your pendant," said Marcus. He hoped Kelvin sensed the sincerity of his apology. "I found it in the alley back in Noam. I planned to give it back, and I would have returned it sooner had I known how much it means to you. Please believe me."

Kelvin said nothing, and Marcus worried that he might not be forgiven. But after a few moments, Kelvin spoke. "It was my mother's," he said. "She died when I was barely a year old. This pendant is all I have of her."

Marcus knew the pain of being orphaned and the longing a child feels for a mother long since dead. "I'm truly sorry," he said. While the crystal had been in his possession, Marcus had only looked at it briefly. But now, seeing it in Kelvin's hand, he noticed its beauty as if for the first time. "It's Celestine, isn't it?" Marcus asked. "It must be worth a small fortune."

Kelvin nodded. "That's why I keep it hidden. But for me its value is beyond price," he said, tucking the pendant into his shirt.

"It's not just the pendant, you know," Kelvin continued. "You've kept things from me, lied to me. You care only for yourself. I cannot forgive you for that. We are both here for one purpose, to find the Rock of Ivanore. You can wait for Jayson if you wish, but I have no more need of him—or of you."

Kelvin's words cut deeply. Now that they were in Dokur, Marcus found himself wanting more than ever to confide in Kelvin, to tell him the truth about Jayson, but a glimpse of a familiar face in the crowd stopped him.

"Look!" he said, discreetly pointing. "It's Arik!"

Forty-one

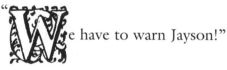e have to warn Jayson!"

Marcus's words were urgent. Jayson had kept his identity secret and had traversed across the entire island to deliver a message he claimed could save Imaness. Now Arik, the man who seemed bent on stopping him, was right here in Dokur.

"You're right, of course," said Kelvin reluctantly. "But first we need to know what Arik is up to. Wait inside. I'll be back soon." Kelvin stealthily threaded his way into the crowd and fell in a few yards behind Arik. Soon they were both out of sight.

Marcus pushed open the tavern's heavy wooden door and allowed his eyes to adjust to the dim light. The room was full of people. Men and women occupied nearly every table in the place, and several servers bustled through the crowded room, delivering plates piled high with food. One server in particular caught Marcus's attention. Her hair, which flowed across her shoulders like a river of black onyx, shimmered in the firelight. He guessed she was four or five years older than he, but that fact seemed trivial compared to her beauty.

A large, dirty man shoved Marcus so hard he nearly fell on his back.

"Outa my way, boy!" said the man, swinging a half-empty wine bottle in his fist. Marcus stepped away from the door and sat at an empty table near the kitchen. The dark-haired server plopped a plate laden with food in front of Marcus with a loud clink.

"Ale?" she asked, filling a mug from a ceramic pitcher. The server placed the mug in front of him, and he drank from it greedily. When he set down the empty mug, she smiled at him. Marcus noticed that her eyes were as bright green as a grassy field in spring.

"Been traveling?" she asked, refilling his mug.

"Yes," he said, suddenly aware of his unkempt appearance. The smell of sweet potatoes and roasted lamb made his stomach grumble. "This looks delicious."

"Well, it does fill an empty stomach," she replied.

A large, round woman appeared at the kitchen door. "Mouse!" she bellowed, wiping her pudgy hands on her apron. "Come get the pies out of the oven!"

The server grinned apologetically. "That's me," she

said as she started for the kitchen. "If you need anything more, just wave. I'll see you."

Several minutes passed with an array of people going in and out of the tavern. Marcus watched apprehensively, hoping that none of them would be Arik. He bided his time by practicing magic with small, inconspicuous tricks such as levitating his fork by condensing the molecules of air beneath it and warming some food that had grown cold. He even managed to get a chair to move several inches, though when the man who had been sitting in it sat down again, he landed on the floor. Marcus stifled a chuckle and went back to his meal.

Xerxes, who had until now been silent, shook his head. "Magic is not for sport," he said disapprovingly.

By the time Kelvin returned, Marcus had cleaned his plate.

"I followed Arik across town to the Dragon's Head Inn," said Kelvin, breathless. "Tristan and Zody are being watched by the Mardoks there."

"What about Clovis?" asked Marcus, alarmed.

"Clovis, too. I heard Arik order one Mardok to take them all upstairs."

"We have to help them," said Marcus.

The server called Mouse came to the table with a plate for Kelvin. She held out a mug and began filling it with ale. Kelvin gave Marcus a wary glance and lowered his voice. "That's not all," said Kelvin. "I also heard Arik say that he and the other Mardoks were going to the watchtower."

"Jayson told me that he had to warn Lord Fredric about

something important," added Marcus, "something that threatened all of Imaness. Could this be what he meant?"

Mouse set the mug on the table. She took up Marcus's empty plate and wiped the table with a dishcloth.

"We have to get word to Jayson at the Fortress," said Marcus, rising from the table.

"I'll go," said Kelvin.

"No, you're much better than I am with a weapon. Free Clovis and the others. I'll find Jayson."

"All right, but be careful!" Kelvin took out his dagger. "Arrows are too dangerous in this crowd," he said, slinging the crossbow across his back. He stood to leave but paused. "Find Bryn, too, will you?"

Kelvin hurried out of the tavern, leaving his untouched food and ale behind.

Marcus reached into his satchel for a handful of coins and dropped them onto the table. "Thank you for your hospitality," he said to Mouse.

"You're going to the Fortress," she said.

A cold chill went through Marcus as he realized that his conversation had been overheard. He politely excused himself, but Mouse followed him to the door.

"You'll never get into the Fortress alive," she pressed. "The guards will run you through before you get two steps inside the gate."

Marcus drew his cape tightly around him. He longed for the warmth of his home in Quendel, of the casual days that filled his life there. As a boy, he had never imagined such dangers existed in the world, and he felt horribly unprepared to face the challenges he was certain now awaited him.

"I must go," he said. "I think one of my friends is imprisoned there, and another friend is in danger. I have to warn him."

"You mean Jayson?" There was an earnest look in Mouse's eyes. She spoke the name as though it was a prayer.

"Who are you?" asked Marcus. He sensed there must be more to this woman than aprons and dishtowels. "The cook called you 'Mouse.' That's an odd name for a woman."

Mouse lowered her voice. "My name is Kaië. As a child, the Fortress was my home."

"Can you get me safely inside?"

"I'm not called Mouse for nothing." Kaië untied her apron and tossed it to another server as she led Marcus out the door. "I'll take you," she added, "but only on one condition."

"Anything," answered Marcus.

"Tell me about Jayson."

Forty-two

The harsh sounds of the city reverberated against Marcus's skull like a constant crack of thunder, causing his head to sprout a throbbing headache.

Kaië deftly weaved her way through the crowd while Marcus struggled to keep her in sight. When they reached the far end of the square, a sour stench churned his stomach. He covered his nose and mouth with his cape to keep it out.

"What is that smell?" he shouted over the din. "It stinks like rotting cabbage!"

Kaië did not slow her pace but called over her shoulder. "It's the public latrines you smell. The city's waste is emptied into an open pit where it drains through a channel into the sea."

Marcus wanted to tell her how disgusted he felt, but he feared that if he opened his mouth again he might vomit. Instead he hurried to catch up with his guide. Soon they were out of the city, climbing a tall, green hill. He was glad he had Xerxes with him to help with the climb.

With the stench of Dokur's sewers behind them, Marcus uncovered his mouth and drew several deep breaths in succession. The clean, salty air that filled his lungs refreshed him.

Above them loomed the Fortress, a mighty castle built of massive granite blocks. But Marcus was not interested in the Fortress just now. His eyes were locked on the magnificent scene directly below them. There, endless ocean waves laced in foam rolled into shore and gently lapped against the white sand. Only the shadow of the watchtower marred the beauty. Marcus stopped to listen to the lull of the ocean.

"Why are we stopping?" asked Xerxes impatiently. Marcus ignored him. He did not want to answer him in front of Kaië.

"Beautiful, isn't it?" Kaië had stopped her relentless march to stand beside him. "I've spent my entire life in Dokur. The sea has been my companion and confidant. I had hoped one day the sea would bring me my freedom."

They stood for several moments gazing toward the horizon. Marcus thought he saw a dark spot in the distance but could not tell what it was. He strained his eyes, trying to make out more detail, but Kaië tugged on his arm.

"We must hurry," she said as they resumed their climb.

"If Jayson was arrested, he would have been taken directly to Chancellor Prost, keeper of the law."

"Arrested? But he came to warn them!"

"Warn them of what?" asked Kaië. "Please tell me."

"But I swore an oath."

In Marcus's hand, Xerxes shook with annoyance. "This is no time for secrets!" he said. "This girl can be of use to us! You will have to confide in her!"

Kaië stopped and crossed her arms. "I won't lead you another step until you explain what is going on."

Marcus hesitated to reveal the secret with which he had been entrusted, but without Kaië he knew helping Jayson would be impossible. "Dokur is in danger," he began. "Jayson came to warn Lord Fredric, but it seems his enemy, Arik, has already arrived."

"Arik is here in Dokur? What does he plan to do?" she asked.

"I don't know exactly," replied Marcus, "but I think he plans to capture the watchtower."

Kaië's eyes flashed with fear. "Arik must intend to prevent the tower guards from sounding the alarm," she said. She turned hastily, increasing her pace. The distance between them and Dokur grew quickly.

Marcus turned his gaze again toward the sea. The dark spot he had seen before seemed to have swelled to twice its size, but still he could not discern any shape to it. In the harbor, Dokur's navy lay as though asleep, their sails bound tightly against bare masts. The sight of them filled him with foreboding.

Forty-three

The Dragon's Head Inn was a dilapidated nook in the dirtiest part of the city. With its entry located in a dark alleyway, it was the shelter of choice for Dokur's most nefarious individuals.

Kelvin pressed himself against the alley wall, hoping the shadows would conceal him from whomever might gaze down from the second-story window. Earlier he had followed Arik to this place and had even slipped inside and hidden beneath a table. It was here that he had overheard Arik's plans.

All but one Mardok was to accompany Arik to the tower, with the one remaining left to guard Clovis and the others. But in the time it had taken Kelvin to get to

Marcus and back, he could not be sure that Arik and the other Mardoks had not already returned.

Kelvin's hands, moist with apprehension, gripped the handle of his dagger as he slipped through the door. To his surprise, he found the room empty. Even the barkeeper was nowhere to be seen. This time he did not take refuge under a table but made his way toward the staircase at the far side of the bar.

Kelvin crept along, his dagger drawn. Each step caused the floorboards beneath his feet to creak. He paused occasionally to listen for movement in case Arik and the Mardoks were lurking about, but he heard nothing. As he continued past the bar, however, he heard a low groan. Kelvin turned, his dagger held high, ready to strike. On the floor behind the bar lay the barkeeper in a pool of his own blood. The barkeeper groaned again and weakly lifted his hand.

Kelvin sheathed his dagger and tore a strip of cloth from his shirt, hoping to use it to stop the bleeding. As he knelt beside the man, he realized that any attempt at saving his life would be futile. The man struggled for each breath, and his body convulsed uncontrollably. Kelvin took his outstretched hand.

"How are you, my friend?" Kelvin asked softly, forcing a smile.

The man managed a feeble smile of his own. "In death's grasp," he whispered. "I overheard their plan to take the tower! Arik and those monsters . . . seizing the tower . . . a fleet of enemy ships waits beyond the harbor!"

The man fell into a violent fit of coughing, and his breaths became even more labored. "I am the only one who knows."

"Hush, now," Kelvin soothed. "Keep still."

"No!" the man's face twisted in an agonized expression. "You must go to the tower! Warn the guards—or Dokur is lost!"

"But my friends are being held captive upstairs. I must rescue them."

The man grabbed Kelvin's hand and pressed something into his palm. "Free them quickly! Then go to the tower! Swear you'll go to the tower!"

Kelvin opened his fingers. In his hand lay a key. "I swear it," he said.

A tranquil expression eased across the barkeeper's face. Then, with one last breath, he died.

Forty-four

At the top of the hill, two hundred yards or so from the base of the Fortress, Kaïë dropped to her knees behind a large boulder. She pulled Marcus down beside her and put a finger to her lips.

She motioned for him to help her. They leaned their weight against the boulder, and it slid away easily, revealing steps descending deep into the earth. Marcus followed Kaïë, a thin finger of sunlight their only illumination.

Soon they reached the bottom of the steps, but whatever lay ahead of them was hidden in darkness. Marcus's stomach tightened into a knot. He had no choice but to trust Kaïë.

"This tunnel leads to Lord Fredric's private chambers," she explained. "It was built as a means of escape should Dokur ever fall under attack."

"Do you take this route often?" asked Marcus.

"Only once before. The night I followed Ivanore."

Xerxes gasped in surprise. Marcus covered the bird's beak with his hand but, realizing the futility of it, let go.

"That was completely unnecessary!" grumbled Xerxes.

Marcus grasped Kaië's hand and turned her toward him. Through the darkness he could see nothing, but he listened for the sound of her breath.

"Who are you, Kaië?" Marcus shivered. The tunnel was damp and cold. "You know about Jayson, and on your insistence I told you why he came here. Now you say you know Ivanore. Explain this to me."

"My mother was Ivanore's maidservant," Kaië answered. Her breath was steady, certain. Marcus felt it on his face, warming him. "When Mother died, Ivanore became like a new mother to me. When she ran away with Jayson, I went with them. I remained by her side when they were betrayed and dried her tears when Jayson was exiled. Their separation broke her heart."

Kaië's breath faltered and her voice choked, but she regained control. "That night, as she escaped, I followed her through this tunnel. When she realized I was following her, she pleaded with me to remain in Dokur and watch the sea until Jayson returned. I was to tell him where to find her. I swore to her that I would deliver her message, and every day for the past fifteen years I have waited. Now, finally, I will be able to fulfill my promise."

The warmth of Kaië's breath moved away from Marcus, and he heard her footsteps echoing against the stone floor ahead of him.

"Wait," he said. "We need light." He retrieved Zyll's key from his pocket and searched the darkness for warmth. He found it in Kaië. Drawing from it and combining it with his own, he funneled their energy into the key itself. The key began to glow, emitting a gentle light that illuminated the area immediately surrounding them. For a moment, Marcus imagined the world had disappeared and only he and Kaië remained within this solitary sphere of light.

"You haven't told me why Jayson would be arrested," he said, hoping his voice did not betray his thoughts. "You'd think Lord Fredric would reward him for trying to save Dokur. And why did Ivanore run away from her own father?"

Kaië continued walking and Marcus followed. A few short minutes later, a thin line of light appeared directly in front of them. A door! Kaië hurried ahead and glanced through the lit crack.

"Lord Fredric's council room. It's empty." She started to open the door but hesitated. "It was the baby," she said at last.

"Baby?" said Marcus in surprise. "What baby?"

"Ivanore and Jayson's son—Fredric's legal heir," explained Kaië. "On the night Jayson was exiled, Fredric swore he would kill the child the very next morning."

Forty-five

ord Fredric's council chamber was a hexagonal-shaped room with wood-paneled walls reaching three stories in height to a stained glass ceiling. Each wall bore a full-length scarlet banner bearing an image embroidered in gold thread: seals of the royal family. In addition to the door through which they had entered, there were two other doors as well.

"That one leads to the main hall," said Kaië, indicating the door opposite them. Then, pointing to the other, "That door opens to a private stairwell leading to the throne room on the second floor."

The room was lit in colored hues filtering through the fragments of glass in the ceiling. Crimson, sapphire, and golden beams burst like a rainbow in midair. As Kaië passed through this brilliant ray, Marcus caught himself staring at her, for the light cast an aura about her as though she were an angel—the light her halo. Sensing that he had fallen into sudden silence, Kaië stopped and turned to face him. For that moment, as he gazed upon her face, he imagined he had indeed been transported to some heaven.

"Are you coming?" asked Kaië, her face blushing with the unanticipated attention.

"Wait," said Marcus. "I'm confused about what you said. I read in the island's history that Ivanore was kidnapped after Jayson's exile. But you claim that Fredric threatened to kill their baby, so Ivanore ran away."

"That's right," replied Kaië. She headed for the door opposite from where they had entered.

Marcus followed. "So, where is Ivanore now?"

As they approached the door, they heard voices outside the room.

"Someone's coming!" squawked Xerxes. "Hide me! Hide me!"

Kaië and Marcus slipped behind one of the tapestries just as the chamber door opened. A guard entered, posting himself beside the tapestry. Two men followed.

"Is he mad?" said an elderly man wearing scarlet robes. "What could possibly induce him to walk right through these gates knowing his sentence is certain death?"

Kaië whispered into Marcus's ear. "That's Lord Fredric, and the other man is Chancellor Prost."

"It matters not why he has come," said the Chancellor, dabbing the corners of his mouth with a handkerchief.

"His plot to usurp your authority will be foiled soon enough."

Chancellor Prost was thin and frail looking, with a sculpted beard and graying temples. He held his right arm level with his chest. Perched on his arm was a small gray bird with a red band around its leg.

"Plot?" said Lord Fredric. "What plot? He has come alone, has he not? And what of his message concerning an enemy fleet off the coast? What think you of that?"

"If there were ships, our tower guards would sound the alarm. No, your Lordship, Jayson means to deceive you and to take from you your crown."

Kaië took Marcus's hand and squeezed it. Though no words were spoken between them, Marcus knew that she felt the same concern for Jayson that he did.

Lord Fredric continued. "That may be, but even so, I wish to speak with him myself."

Chancellor Prost held up an emaciated hand and pointed his bony finger at Fredric's chest. "I must protest! As the keeper of the law, it is my duty to provide order and protection to you and the entire realm. This man is a criminal! An enemy to Dokur! He deserves no mercy!"

Lord Fredric sat in an ornate chair bearing a royal seal and contemplated the words of his Chancellor. Then he straightened himself and called to the guard.

"Bring in the prisoner."

Forty-six

In the Dragon's Head Inn, Kelvin examined the key the barkeeper had given him. Tied to it was a leather tag with the name of the inn and the number '3' impressed on it. A shadow fell over him. He spun around and thrust his dagger forward, but a massive hand grabbed his wrist. Kelvin's eyes traveled from the hand up a muscular arm covered in coarse hair to a broad, metal-plated chest. The Mardok sneered and tightened its grip on Kelvin's wrist. A needle-like pain shot up his forearm. Kelvin cried out, but with his free hand, he grabbed an arrow from the quiver on his back and jammed its point into the back of the Mardok's hand. The Mardok released its victim, howling in pain, giving Kelvin just enough time to scurry up the stairs.

Kelvin soon found himself at the end of a long, dark hallway lined with doors. The door directly to his right bore the number '12'.

Rapid, heavy footsteps sounded on the staircase. Kelvin ran down the hall. The numbers on the doors grew smaller. He glanced behind him just as the Mardok leapt over the top three stairs and started down the hall after him.

"Almost there!" whispered Kelvin, encouraging himself onward. Finally, to his left he saw a number '3.' He thrust the key into the lock, glancing up only once to see the distance between him and the Mardok shrinking quickly. The lock was stiff; it took all his strength to turn it. Finally the lock clicked and the door gave way. Kelvin slipped into the room and slammed the door shut, locking it behind him. He scanned the room and discovered three pairs of eyes staring at him from the corner.

Tristan, Zody, and Clovis were tied together back to back, their ropes threaded around an iron ring in the floor. Kelvin did not waste a moment. He dashed to their side and began sawing at the ropes with his dagger. Clovis, who faced the wall, strained his neck to see what was happening behind him.

"Kelvin! Thank goodness you've come!" he said.

A tremendous thud shook the room.

"What was that?" asked Tristan.

Kelvin continued to work furiously to free his friends. "Mardok," he said.

Clovis began to whimper.

"Hurry!" urged Tristan, tugging on the shredded portion of rope around his wrists. Within seconds his hands were free, and he rubbed them to get the circulation flowing again.

Another loud thump sounded at the door.

"Don't just stand there!" ordered Kelvin. "Help me free the others!"

Tristan glanced around the room. He spotted the bed, a simple wooden frame with three slats and a feather mattress. After pulling the mattress to the floor, Tristan grabbed the end of the bed frame with both hands. Bracing his legs against the wall, he pulled with all his might. The wood cracked and splintered and finally gave way, leaving a jagged three-foot beam in his hand.

"What are you doing!?" hissed Kelvin, who had just freed Zody and was now working on Clovis. Another thud, much louder than before, thundered through the room along with the sound of splintering wood. Clovis's whimpers turned into sobs.

The door crumbled into a pile of tinder. The Mardok growled and lunged forward for the kill. At that moment, Tristan leaped into the Mardok's path and shoved the wooden beam directly beneath its ribs. The Mardok's momentum and the weight of its body instantly plunged the wood deep into its abdomen. The creature howled in agony just as Clovis was freed from his rope.

"Wonderful!" said Zody. "But now what?"

Kelvin looked up and realized that the injured Mardok still stood between them and the door.

"How are we going to get out?" cried Clovis.

"I'm not going near that thing!" said Zody. The Mardok cried out again, and then its eyes rolled back in its head. Its massive body grew limp and crumpled to the floor in a lifeless heap.

"Is it dead?" asked Tristan.

Kelvin approached cautiously and tested the Mardok's shoulder with his foot. "It's dead! Come on!" He stepped over the Mardok's body and hurried to the doorway. Tristan and Zody followed, but Clovis refused to budge.

"Clovis, you can't stay here!" said Kelvin. "Arik and the other Mardoks could come back any second! Do you really want to be here when they do?"

Clovis shook his head.

"Besides," added Tristan, "if they do find you, guess who'll be the main course for dinner tonight?"

"Here!" said Kelvin. He removed the crossbow and quiver from his back and tossed it to Clovis. Clovis caught it and gasped in surprise.

"My dad's bow!" he said. "I thought I lost—"

"Never mind! You're going to need it if we run across any more Mardoks—which is bound to happen if we don't leave right now!"

Clovis gulped and walked up to the Mardok. Trembling, he closed his eyes and stepped over the assassin's hairy arm. Just then the Mardok's hand reached up and grabbed Clovis by the ankle. "It's got me! It's got me!" Clovis screamed.

Kelvin jumped forward and with one swift strike with his dagger severed the Mardok's hand from its wrist. The Mardok screamed one last time and then went silent.

The four boys did not wait around to see if the beast was really dead this time. They ran as fast as they could down the stairs and out of the Dragon's Head Inn forever.

Forty-seven

In the Fortress's council chambers, Chancellor Prost bowed in compliance with Lord Fredric's command and stepped aside. The door opened and a guard entered, a heavy chain in his hands. Attached to the chain was a pair of iron cuffs clasped around Jayson's wrists. Jayson carried himself proudly, even though his body bore signs of a beating. On his cheek was an open gash still red with blood, and his arms were covered with purple bruises. Marcus cursed himself for letting Jayson come alone.

Xerxes, who was wedged between Marcus and Kaië, complained. "Drat this tapestry! I can't see a thing!"

"Shhh!" whispered Marcus.

Kaië looked at him, a question on her face. With so few options available at the moment, Marcus simply shrugged.

Lord Fredric leaned back in his chair and scrutinized his prisoner. "Has it really been fifteen years since we last met?" he said. His voice sounded sad and weary, not at all like the powerful leader Marcus had envisioned. "How strange it is that time marches on despite all our efforts to stop it. What I wouldn't give to turn back the years if only I could."

"I am not interested in the past," said Jayson. Though in obvious pain, his gaze bore down on his captor like leaden weights. "The past is dead to me."

"Dead, you say?" replied Lord Fredric. "So Ivanore means nothing to you. Your son means nothing."

"That's a lie!" shouted Jayson. "My wife and child are the very air that I breathe! My heart would have ceased beating long ago if it were not for my memories of them. No, it is my resentment of the past that is dead, the pain you caused me that I have forgotten. That is why I have come to warn you of danger."

"What danger have I to fear?" Fredric laughed cynically. "If a tidal wave were to destroy my home, my land, my very life, I would be grateful! But no, my lungs are compelled to keep breathing, my heart to keep beating— though I have willed them a thousand times to stop! No, Jayson, if what you say is true, that an enemy awaits to conquer Dokur, then I welcome him!"

"Surely you must wish to defend your people? To defend Ivanore and your grandson!"

Lord Fredric's gaze drifted, and Marcus noted how his eyes seemed moist. "How can I defend them?" Fredric continued wearily. "Ivanore disappeared the night I exiled you. I have been searching for my daughter these many years and have never found her." He stood with effort and walked toward the center of the room until he stood in the cascade of color. "Every day, when the sun sets upon the sea, I die a little more, knowing that she is gone from me."

"She never returned?" said Jayson, his voice taut with disbelief.

"No, though for many years I believed she had joined you in Hestoria. But now that you are here, I see this is not so."

Jayson pulled at his chains, his muscles straining. The guards pulled him back, nearly knocking him off balance. "All this time I thought Ivanore was here in Dokur preparing our son to lead his people one day!" he said angrily. "I stayed away because I thought it best for my son to never know his father was of mixed blood. And now you tell me they are lost?"

A guard struck Jayson in the chest with the blunt end of his sword. He doubled over in pain and dropped to his knees. Marcus struggled against an overwhelming desire to come to his defense, but he knew that revealing himself now would only jeopardize them both.

Once Jayson caught his breath, he looked up into Fredric's eyes, pleading. "Why did she run away?" he whispered.

Fredric turned his back to him. "I am ashamed to say it."

Jayson shouted. "I demand that you tell me!"

"I am an old man," began Fredric haltingly, "and the years have softened me. But when I was a younger man, I guarded my position greedily. When my daughter married you against my wishes—you, a man of Agoran descent—I was outraged. I wanted to execute you, but my daughter pleaded for your life. So instead I sent you away. What you did not know was the extent of my jealousy and hatred of you."

Fredric stepped out of the rainbow of light into the darker hues of the room. "The night of your exile I threatened to destroy the child. I looked on him as a mongrel, and I cursed him for his impure blood. I was angry! My words were impulsive! You cannot know how deeply I regret them now. No doubt fearing for her child's life, Ivanore ran away. I have not seen her since that night."

He lowered himself into his chair and let out a low, pitiful sigh. His hands, crooked and swollen with age, clenched the armrests. "I will soon pass from this world," he said with resignation. "I have no heir, and the realm will become subject to anarchy. Perhaps it is better to be conquered by our enemy than to disintegrate into chaos."

"You have an heir," said Jayson. "Will you not mention his name?"

"My son is dead to me!" Fredric's voice exploded with a force of which no one in the room thought he was capable. But the outburst took its toll, leaving his limbs trembling. He continued with restrained emotion. "I do not wish to speak anymore of treachery. I am feeling ill and will retire to my chambers."

Jayson tried to stand. The guard jerked him back with his chains, but Jayson could not be swayed. "Don't you know what your hatred has done?" Jayson said. "You have driven your son to treason! Arik is behind this invasion. The scroll I bring with me testifies of it. It contains the ancient map of the Black Forest, as well as details of the invasion—written in his own hand."

A guard presented the scroll to Fredric, who read it silently. "My son . . . declares war on Dokur?" he said finally.

"Yes," answered Jayson. "And you can hate him for that as well—or you can make your peace with him and possibly save Dokur."

Lord Fredric remained silent for several minutes. When he did speak again, it was with the voice of a man whose soul bore a heavy burden. "Should Arik come to me, I will pardon him. But it seems that events are already in motion and war is inevitable. Yet I cannot defend Dokur," said Fredric. "As you know, we have not been attacked in nearly a century. We have become apathetic. Our navy is manned with only minimal forces. Our army is scattered throughout the land. If our enemy comes by sea, as you say he will, and the tower is breached and captured, we have no way to signal our troops in the neighboring valleys. Even if we could contact them, it would take days to gather an army sufficient for battle. All is lost."

Jayson lowered his head, his chest and shoulders expanding and contracting in steady rhythm with his breathing. There was silence in the room, a heavy silence that felt to Marcus as a millstone about the neck of Dokur.

"How many slaves work in the mines?" asked Jayson, raising his face to look at Lord Fredric. When no answer was given, he spoke again. "I know what you have done to my people. I have seen the mine with my own eyes. Now, tell me—how many are there?"

Lord Fredric looked to Chancellor Prost for the answer.

"We have four hundred Agoran and two dozen armed human guards," said the Chancellor. He stepped forward until he stood over Jayson. The bird with the red band cooed contentedly on his arm. "Are you suggesting we place weapons in the hands of slaves?"

"If we were to release them, surely they would join our enemies," said Fredric. "Or they would flee."

Jayson rose to his feet, his chains clinking loudly. "This is their land, as well. The Agoran are a proud people. Give them their freedom, and they will fight."

Chancellor Prost guffawed. "Give them their freedom?! You *are* mad!"

"Free them—or be destroyed. There is no other option."

Prost opened his mouth to protest again, but Lord Fredric held up his hand to silence him. "I have been their captor. They will not follow me," he said.

"I will lead them," said Jayson.

Prost's face grew crimson, yet he held his tongue in check as Lord Fredric ordered the guards to release Jayson from his bonds. As the chains fell to the floor in a loud clatter, Jayson knelt before his king. Fredric, visibly moved by his action, bade him to rise. Then he spoke to the guards. "Arnot, Thyren, you will accompany this man. Gather weapons from the armory." Then to Jayson he said, "You must go to the mines immediately. Tell your people they are free. You will need proof of my declaration. My seal, perhaps?"

"I will show them this," said Jayson. He reached into the pouch at his waist and retrieved a flat object the size of his palm, a half-circle of sea-colored crystal. Though the design on it was broken, Marcus recognized it immediately as the same seal that appeared on the banner behind which he stood.

Fredric's eyes widened when he saw it. "Ivanore's royal seal!"

Jayson ran his fingers over the embossed design. "She broke it in two and gave half of it to me before we were separated," he said. "She said it was to remind me that my other half waited here until the day we could be reunited."

Fredric reached out his withered hand and wrapped it around Jayson's hand, clasping the seal. "Perhaps, if the gods be willing, this may still come to pass. Now go swiftly. Take my guards with you. Bring back whatever army you can gather," he said, "and pray we may all live to see another day."

Forty-eight

Lord Fredric excused himself from the council chambers, leaving Prost to oversee Jayson's departure for the mines. Prost ordered fresh supplies along with Fredric's fastest horses. The two guards assigned to Jayson were given the charge to protect him at all costs—and to see to it that the authorities at the mine heeded his message.

"The mine keeper is a disagreeable fellow," warned Prost, "but with Ivanore's seal at your disposal, you should have little trouble convincing him of your authority, though I think it wise to carry Lord Fredric's banner, as well."

Jayson nodded his thanks and headed for the door, anxious to be on his way. It was nearing midday and time would not keep.

"One more thing," added Prost, his voice laced with feigned empathy, "I do apologize for Fredric's earlier outburst about his son, but you must comprehend the position Arik has put him in."

"Arik acted out of grief from a father's loathing of him," replied Jayson. "What he's done is a terrible thing, but you heard Fredric same as I did. Arik need only admit his wrongdoing, and he will be forgiven."

Prost preened his bird's feathers with his fingertips, a cunning smile on his lips. "And will *you* forgive Arik as well?"

"There is nothing to forgive."

"Then you don't know," added Prost, his eyes widening with mock innocence.

"What are you talking about?" Jayson was becoming impatient.

The bird walked up Prost's arm to his shoulder and snuggled against his chin. "That Arik told Fredric where you and Ivanore were hiding, of course," said Prost. "It was he who betrayed you those many years ago."

Jayson's expression did not reveal anger or surprise. He did not have time to concern himself about a friendship that was already lost. Instead he turned his back on Prost and left to get on with his duty. Thyren followed.

Outside the chamber door, beyond Marcus and Kaië's hearing, Arnot awaited his final orders. Prost gave them. "It would be a tragedy if Jayson and Arik died in battle," he said. "See to it, won't you?"

Forty-nine

Finding the council chambers finally empty, Kaië and Marcus slipped out from behind the tapestry. Kaië hurried across the room to the tunnel's door, but Marcus stopped her.

"I can't leave yet," he told her. "Yesterday a friend of mine was captured by Lord Fredric's soldiers—a little boy. I have to find him."

"Can't leave? Can't leave?" squealed Xerxes.

Marcus tried his best to ignore him. "I have to get him out of here or he'll be executed."

"The holding cells are located in the lower levels of the Fortress," said Kaië. "Their entrance is on the opposite side of the main corridor, but they are under heavy guard. You won't get through undetected."

Marcus looked around the room, searching for something he could use to disguise himself, but found nothing useful.

Again Xerxes protested. "I'm not going to any prison cell! I demand we leave this place immediately!"

Marcus opened the door a crack and peered into the corridor. He saw a long, wide hall supported by massive stone arches. At the far end was a narrow, wooden door barred with a solid beam.

"There are guards posted everywhere," whispered Marcus. He felt in his pocket for the key and considered his options. Magic was limited to manipulating the elements of the earth, he reminded himself. He could not conjure something out of thin air.

"Maybe I could create a distraction," he suggested out loud.

"What sort of distraction?" asked Kaië.

"Something that would draw away the guards long enough for us to reach the prison."

Xerxes voice was irate now. "I won't be a party to your killing us all! No, I'll have none of it!" Then he went silent, reverting to his wooden self.

Marcus was too concerned about his present situation to worry about Xerxes. He thought of Bryn locked away behind that wooden door. As Marcus contemplated the possible punishments he might already have suffered, the key's temperature rose in his hand. He knew he had one chance to get by the guards. One chance only.

The key now burned against his flesh. He held it up and focused his thoughts. Beneath him, the stone floor began to tremble. The entire room shook with such great violence that objects on Lord Fredric's desk wobbled and fell to the floor. Shouts emanated from the hall, and the sound of running footsteps grew distant.

Marcus peered through the door once again. The quake was stronger than he had anticipated, but it had worked. The hall was empty. "The soldiers are gone," he announced. "Let's hurry before they come back."

A peculiar weakness seized Marcus following the quake. But though it alarmed him, he said nothing. He and Kaië ran down the hall toward the entrance to the lower levels. They listened to the confused and fearful voices of the soldiers outside. Marcus was out of breath by the time they reached the opposite end of the hall, the magic having drained him of strength. He and Kaië pushed against the beam across the door. In his weakened state, Marcus could only muster minimal effort, but with a few forceful shoves, it gave way.

"We don't have much time," said Kaië, sprinting down the steps into the cold, damp darkness below. The steps seemed to descend forever, and Marcus fought against the familiar fear that gripped him. He wondered whether they would ever reach the bottom, when suddenly he found himself on level ground. Water trickled down the walls of the chamber, and the dank stench of mildew invaded his nostrils. A single torch scarcely illuminated the area, leaving much of it in shadow.

"Bryn!" Marcus called out. He felt his strength returning. "Bryn! Are you here?" The clanking of irons and the moans of someone roused from sleep broke the silence.

"Who is there?" a voice, weak and strained, called back. Marcus peered into the cell beside him and saw the silhouette of a scrawny man with a shaggy, unkempt beard.

"I'm searching for someone who was taken captive yesterday," said Marcus.

"You mean the boy?" replied the man, coming to the bars of his cell. "They put him in the last chamber. We two are the only inhabitants of this hell today."

In the dim light, Marcus could now clearly make out the prisoner's face. "You're Agoran," he said.

The prisoner nodded. "I am Eliha."

Marcus thanked Eliha and felt his way down to the end of the hall, leaving Kaië beside the stairwell. His heart pounded furiously as he called Bryn's name once more. This time he received the response he had been hoping for.

Fifty

"**M**arcus! You have come for me?" Bryn's tearful voice called out through the darkness.

Marcus held the key up to the cell door and commanded the lock to turn. When the cell door opened, Bryn stumbled out and fell upon Marcus, sobbing. "Why do you risk so much to save me?"

"You did as much for me and Kelvin," replied Marcus. "But we have to hurry or we may all spend eternity down here together."

The Agoran, Eliha, reached through his cell bars and grasped Marcus's cape as he hurried by. "Free me as well!" he pleaded.

"I can't free a criminal," said Marcus, pulling away from the prisoner's grasp.

"I am no criminal! I was taken from my family to work in the mines. I escaped and tried to get back to my wife and my three children, but I was captured, beaten, and thrown in this hellish pit. Please, I beg of you!"

Knowing that the guards would soon be returning to their posts, Marcus wanted to get out of that place as quickly as possible, but his conscience would not let him leave another living soul to suffer in this place alone. He held the key close to the lock. The latch within clicked open as before. Eliha flew out of the cell, pushed past Marcus and ran up the stairs. Halfway up he stopped and turned back.

"Hurry!" he said impatiently.

The four of them reached the top step and paused at the door.

"Once we open it," said Kaië, "the guards will know we're here."

"Then we should be as subtle as possible." Marcus held up the key. He focused on opening the door with a gentle push of air, but his anxiety surged into the key, and in a powerful burst of energy, the door exploded off its hinges and skidded across the hall, taking three soldiers by surprise.

"Well," said Marcus as the soldiers turned and faced them, "I say we run!"

Marcus, Kaië, and the others sped through the doorway back toward the council chambers, but the guards blocked the way, their swords drawn.

"Up here!" shouted Kaië. The group turned back the way they came, heading for the flight of stairs leading up to the second floor of the Fortress.

"Where are we going?" shouted Bryn.

Kaië did not respond but continued down the hall at the top of the stairs. Marcus knew immediately what she intended to do. She was heading for the throne room and from there down the private steps to the council chambers and out through the tunnel. They reached the second floor and found themselves in front of a massive, ornately carved wooden door. Surely this must be the entrance to the throne room, thought Marcus, relieved that they would get out alive after all.

Suddenly two armed guards stepped between them and the door.

Marcus drew his sword and managed to injure one of them. But his full strength had not yet returned, and the confrontation weakened him even more. The other guard struck at him; Marcus barely warded off the blow.

Two more guards came up behind them, having followed them from the first floor. Marcus, Kaië, Bryn, and Eliha found themselves surrounded.

"I'm sorry, Bryn," said Marcus. It was all he could think of to say. He considered using magic to fight the guards, though he feared doing so might leave him without the strength to escape. Magic is my only choice, he thought. But as he held out the key, the guard to his left struck him with the butt of his sword. The key flew from Marcus's hand and clattered across the floor.

Marcus was relieved that the soldier had not noticed the key, and he determined a way to get it back. But with each passing moment, the soldiers tightened their circle around him. There are too many of them, he thought.

Just when it appeared that he and the others would be forced to surrender, Bryn grabbed the nearest soldier by the arm. With a surge of inhuman strength, he flung the stunned man against the wall. Marcus watched, horrified, as the small boy who had been his companion, his enemy, and his friend for the past five days mutated into a grotesque monster. Black hair sprouted across his back and arms. His torso stretched to four times the boy's normal height, and his face contorted into that of a ferocious fanged beast. The Groc threw back its head and howled. The guards screamed in terror. Even Kaië and the Agoran prisoner huddled together, trembling in fear.

Marcus watched as Bryn, wielding dagger-like claws, dispatched another guard in a single blow. But the shouts of a dozen more guards from below told him that Bryn would soon be outnumbered.

"Hurry!" shouted Kaië, pointing toward the throne room door. "If we go now, we'll make it!"

She grabbed Marcus by the hand and pulled him through the doorway, with the Agoran close behind. The Groc ran to the door but did not pass through. Instead he turned to face the advancing soldiers.

"Go!" he shouted. Bryn's low, animal-like voice no longer bore the soft, high pitch of the child's form he held before. "I will keep them from following you!"

"No, Bryn!" answered Marcus. "You can't fight all of them! They'll kill you!"

Bryn turned to Marcus. Behind him Marcus could see the soldiers running down the hall, the blades of their swords hungry for blood.

"You are my friend," Bryn said. "It is an honor to die for a friend." Then Bryn grabbed the edge of the door with his claws and pulled it shut. Marcus ran to it, flinging his fists against the wood.

"No! Bryn! No!" Through the door he could hear Bryn's roar and the soldiers' screams. A loud piercing howl tore through him, and then all went silent. Someone grabbed Marcus from behind and pulled him through the throne room, down a flight of stairs, and into a dark tunnel. He didn't pay attention to what was around him; all he could think of was Bryn. It wasn't until daylight struck his eyes that he realized he and Kaië and the Agoran were free. They had emerged at the end of the tunnel on the side of a grassy hill overlooking the ocean. Bryn—and the key—were gone.

Fifty-one

On horseback, the distance from Dokur to the mines took little more than an hour. Jayson arrived flanked by Lord Fredric's two guards, Thyren and Arnot.

The three men approached the guard post, a small wooden structure situated on an outcropping of rock overlooking the mine. A sentry stood warming his hands before a small fire. He was a stout fellow with a mass of disheveled hair on his head and chin. A dull plate of metal covered his chest, and a leather whip curled into a loop hung at his waist.

"What do you want?" he asked.

Thyren spoke first. "We are sent by Lord Fredric of Dokur with a message for Sergeant Damen."

"I'm Damen. What's the message?"

Jayson handed the sentry a rolled piece of parchment sealed with wax. Damen cracked the seal and read over the scroll.

"Dokur is under siege," said Jayson. "We haven't time to gather troops. Lord Fredric commands you to free the slaves."

Damen's lips spread into a jeering grin. "Which of you is in charge?"

"I am," said Jayson.

Damen glared at Jayson with contempt and spat on the ground. Then he rolled up the parchment, tucked it underneath his arm, and began to walk away.

Thyren dismounted and caught Damen by the shoulder, turning him around. "You will obey these orders, sir!"

Damen shouted, waving a finger at Jayson. "I'll take no orders from the likes of *him*. That mongrel belongs in the mine with the rest of his kind."

In half a breath's time, Thyren drew his sword and had the point of it pressed behind Damen's left ear. A sheath of perspiration formed along the sergeant's forehead. "You will take his orders," he said, "or I will see to it that you never hear any orders again!"

With a noticeable gulp, Damen nodded and turned his full attention to Jayson.

"Dokur is in danger," continued Jayson. "We need soldiers immediately. You are to free the slaves and distribute the weapons from this wagon."

"Give them weapons?! Are you insane? They would kill me and all the other guards the moment a blade is placed in their hands!"

In one swift motion, Jayson reached down from his horse and grabbed Damen by the collar, lifting him several inches into the air. "Killing you would be more than you deserve, you rotten parasite! I have known your kind, and I have killed them without a second thought. The world would be better off without you. Lord Fredric has promised these men their freedom in exchange for their loyalty, and I will wager any one of them would gladly risk his life for such an offer. You, on the other hand, would rather cower behind a child than lift your sword in battle. Now, you will call the slaves together and instruct your men to fulfill his Lordship's orders, or I will gladly let the slaves have their way with you before we go."

Damen's body shuddered as Jayson let him fall to the ground. The sergeant scrambled to his feet and ran to the guard post. A loud horn sounded. The slaves laid down their tools and assembled in a wide, flat area just below them. Though the men were lean in stature, they were fierce looking, hardened from many years in the mines.

"Speak loudly and slowly," instructed Damen. "The walls of the canyon naturally amplify your voice."

Jayson stood before the silent throng and looked from one angry face to another. These were his people, his brothers, and his friends.

"Agorans," he began, searching for the right words, "I bring you a message from Dokur. An enemy fleet off the coast is preparing to attack. Our army is scattered and cannot be organized in time. Dokur's survival rests on you."

A low rumble rose up from the crowd. One man stepped forward. He stood a foot taller than most of the others, and though he was obviously young, the scars across his back revealed a strong and proud will. "Impossible!" he shouted. "No enemy can approach Dokur undetected!"

"The tower has been compromised," explained Jayson. "Lord Fredric has commanded that you be given weapons and asks that you come to Dokur's defense."

"Fredric?" scoffed the tall slave. "He is the one responsible for these scars on my back. He tore our wives and children from our arms and drove them to the marshlands like cattle! Tell Fredric that we slaves will gladly take his weapons and will use them to exact revenge upon him!"

Jayson waited for the crowd to quiet down before he continued. "What is your name?" he asked the man, obviously the leader of the group. The slave spoke with such courage, such ferocity, that Jayson could not help but respect him.

"My name is Nathar," said the slave, "and you can tell that scoundrel Fredric that we would love nothing better than to see Dokur in ruins!"

"That would not be wise, my friend," replied Jayson, "since Dokur's fate will be yours as well. His Lordship has promised you your freedom if you join him in battle. He also guarantees that the land you once called home will be home again. Your families may return, and the Agorans and humans will live in peace."

"Lies!" said Nathar, shaking his fist in the air.

"Not lies!" Jayson responded. "The truth! I have spoken with Fredric myself. He has given me his word."

"Who are you that we should believe you?"

Jayson hesitated. He had broken the law by marrying a human and siring a child by her. He alone was responsible for Fredric's loathing of the Agoran people. For fifteen years he had remained exiled and had made no attempt to stop the atrocities committed against his people. The guilt of it rested heavily on him, and now as he stood before these men, he feared that the vision he had laid out for Fredric may have been overly optimistic. They might very well blame him for their hardships and the accusation would be justified. How could he ask them to follow him? How could they trust him to lead them?

Jayson faced them boldly. He thought of the last time he had seen his infant son as he held him in his arms and kissed him good-bye. The memory gave him courage. For him, Jayson would do everything possible to save Dokur— to save his people.

He took Ivanore's seal from his pouch and clasped it tightly between his fingers. It would prove him true should anyone doubt him. "I am Jayson!" he shouted so that his name echoed against the walls of the canyon. "And I have returned to lead you out of bondage!"

The crowd fell silent. They knew him; he could see it in their eyes. But could they forgive him? Would they trust him?

A roar of shouts erupted from the mass of slaves. Some fell to their knees, thanking the gods for deliverance. Others called out pledges of loyalty to the man who had defied Lord Fredric and lived.

Jayson took Fredric's banner from Arnot's hands and
drew a burning stick from the fire. With the charred end
of it he wrote on the back of the banner:

FOR OUR FAMILIES
OUR LAND
AND OUR LIBERTY

Then he held the banner high above his head for all
to see.

The crowd broke into frantic cheering and rushed
forward to claim their weapons. When the wagon was
empty, the remaining men returned for their picks and
shovels and hammers.

The last man to the wagon was Nathar, the tall, out-
spoken slave. He stood before Jayson with his head
bowed. "Forgive my disrespect," he said. "I did not know
who you were. My family is dead. I have nothing to live
for, but if my blood be spilt to give these men a chance to
be reunited with their loved ones, then I give it freely."

Jayson laid his hand firmly on Nathar's shoulder. "You
are a good leader, my friend. You know these men, and
they will follow you. Take this," he said, handing Fredric's
banner to Nathar. "Ride before them. Give them courage.
Will you do that for me?"

Nathar nodded, his eyes moist with gratitude. Jayson
called to Damen to bring a horse. Nathar mounted it and
straightened his scarred back. Then, as he held the banner
high, the slaves fell into ranks behind him.

Fifty-two

Morning had melted into midday by the time Marcus and Kaië emerged from the tunnel entrance. The Agoran, Eliha, placed a grateful hand on Marcus's shoulder.

"I thank you," he said, "and I am sorry for the loss of your friend." With that, Eliha scuttled off, soon disappearing from sight.

Marcus squinted his eyes as they adjusted to the bright sun, shining directly overhead. The reality of what had just occurred settled on him like a lead weight. He had never before felt such despair. But he did not even have time to mourn for Bryn, nor for the loss of Zyll's key.

Kaië pointed toward the sea. What Marcus saw there alarmed him. Just beyond the harbor was a fleet of ships.

Above each one, Hestoria's blue-and-black flag flapped in the wind. Years earlier, relations between Hestoria and Dokur had grown cold after a band of Hestorian spies broke into the royal vaults, making off with several items—including an ancient map drawn by the island's earliest settlers. Lord Fredric ended trade with the mainland and prepared for war. As the years passed with no confrontation, however, Lord Fredric and his people grew apathetic. But now several dozen Hestorian ships were approaching, enemy soldiers standing ready on their decks.

On the decks of Dokur's own ships, groups of worried sailors stared toward the horizon, the realization of danger only now becoming apparent. On the cliffs above the shore, citizens of Dokur gathered to see the approaching ships for themselves.

"What do we do?" asked Kaië.

Marcus silently observed the advancing ships. If Jayson did not return with the slave army by nightfall, Dokur would be crushed, and all of Imaness would be in danger of invasion.

In his hands, Xerxes sprang to life and gasped. "We're under attack!" he screeched. "Quick, Marcus, the key! Send a tidal wave down on those Hestorian swine!"

"I can't," Marcus whispered.

"What do you mean *can't?*"

"I lost it in the Fortress."

Xerxes gasped again, louder than before. His beaked clicked angrily. "You can't be serious! How irresponsible!

How careless! Zyll will certainly have something to say—"

Marcus grasped Xerxes' head and drew the blade, fastening the empty staff beneath his cape.

"I don't have time to argue now!" he said, gripping Xerxes so hard that the muscles in his arms and shoulders grew taut. His feet moved faster and faster as he ran across the hill toward the rocky shore. Kaië called after him.

"Marcus! Stop!" But the roar of the waves and the sound of blood pounding through his body drowned out all other sounds. Ahead of him, the Eye of Dokur pierced the sky, gazing down on him like a condescending god. As he neared, a new voice echoed in his ears.

"Marcus! Marcus!"

Marcus slowed to a stop. The voice called again, and the familiar face of Clovis Dungham appeared from behind a jagged boulder not far from the base of the tower. Holding a finger to his lips, he gestured for Marcus to come closer.

"Clovis, you're free," said Marcus, kneeling beside his friend in the sand. Zody and Tristan were with him. "Are you all right?"

"A bit hungry actually, but fine," replied Clovis. "Have you seen Kelvin?"

"Isn't he with you?"

"He was," replied Tristan, "but after we escaped from the Mardok, he said he had to hurry to the tower. He told us to wait here until he returned."

"How long have you been waiting?" Marcus asked.

"Not long," said Zody. "Half an hour, at most."

By this time, Kaië had caught up with Marcus. Out of breath, she chastised him for running ahead. "If this is a race, I gladly concede," she said, panting.

After Marcus made hasty introductions, he explained to everyone present about Arik's role in the impending attack from the sea, Jayson's meeting with Lord Fredric, and his call to bring the Agoran slaves back to Dokur.

"But why did Kelvin go to the tower?" asked Tristan. "He can't fight Arik alone!"

"No, he can't," said Marcus, brandishing his sword in the sunlight. "I'm going to join him."

"We'll come, too," said Clovis.

"There's no sense in that! You don't have any weapons!"

"I have my bow," Clovis replied, but Marcus shook his head.

"I can manage fine on my own," he insisted. "Go with Kaië. Get the word out to the villagers of Arik's intentions, and see if you can get them to fight. By the looks of that fleet, we'll be invaded before nightfall."

Marcus turned back toward the tower and tried to determine the best approach so as not to be seen. The tower stood in the center of a large outcropping of rock just above the sand. There was nothing behind which he could hide. He would have to approach in plain view.

He watched as Kaië led Tristan, Clovis, and Zody back to the crest of the hill beyond which stood the Fortress, and past that, Dokur. At the top of the hill, Kaië paused and looked over her shoulder. Her face wore a troubled expression. The sight of it was forever impressed on Marcus's mind. Then she was gone.

Marcus turned his attention to the tower. Thinking of Bryn and Jayson, a powerful energy welled within him. With his sword held tightly in his hands, he sprinted across the sand. An armed Mardok met him at the base of the tower, their swords clashing as they struck one another. But the Mardok was no match for Marcus, whose sudden surge of strength surprised them both. He did not have time to contemplate what source had fueled his power. Marcus left the wounded Mardok where he lay and hurried into the tower.

Inside, a steep staircase spiraled up the interior walls. Marcus climbed them with ease, taking two and three steps at a time. He had climbed halfway to the top when a second Mardok appeared above him. The creature hurled a dagger at him, which caught him by surprise. As Marcus twisted to avoid contact with the blade, he lost his balance and fell from the precarious ledge on which he stood. Only his quick impulse to grab hold of the edge saved him. The Mardok, on seeing his failure, ran down the stairs toward Marcus. Marcus pulled himself to safety just as the Mardok descended on him. Marcus thrust his sword forward, but the Mardok slipped to the side, sending his own sword down like thunder on the stone steps. They exchanged blow after blow until finally Marcus landed a successful strike to the Mardok's chest. The creature bellowed in pain and toppled from the ledge to the hard, cold floor below.

Marcus ascended the remaining steps to a door at the top. The door was slightly ajar, and as he approached, he heard a voice.

"Come in, Marcus," it said. "I have been expecting you."

Fifty-three

As Kaië led Clovis, Tristan, and Zody away from the beach, Dokur's navy ships sprang to life. Whistles blew and men shouted orders. Canons were stripped of their dusty covers, and sails were freed from their bonds. The sight of Hestoria's fleet weighing anchor outside the harbor had sent them into a confused frenzy. But it was what they saw next that turned their confusion into terror.

On the deck of each enemy ship, a dark mass appeared, rising from below deck. As the formless masses unfurled their wings, stretching out their long and thorny necks, the air split with their deep, bellowing calls.

Dragons!

The first dragon flapped its wings, lifting its immense body into the air. Soon the others took flight, as well. The people on the cliffs screamed and fled in terror.

Kaië watched as the swarm of dragons flew across the harbor toward the anchored navy. The first dragon opened its jaws, and a tongue of flame lashed out, igniting the bow of one of the ships. The men on board scurried to douse the fire, only to be buffeted by more dragons. Within a few short minutes, the entire fleet of Dokur was in flames.

"We must find shelter!" shouted Kaië as she led the three boys over the hill below the Fortress. Behind them the cries of men in pain mingled with the dragons' calls. Soon they reached the secret tunnel. "You'll be safe here," Kaië told them. "I'm going to warn the other citizens."

"You're coming back, right?" asked Zody.

Kaië shook her head. "I must fight alongside my people."

"Let us fight with you," said Tristan.

Zody interrupted. "Tristan, have you lost your mind? There are *dragons* out there! And Arik took our weapons, remember?"

"I have a weapon." Clovis proudly held up his crossbow. "I'll go with Kaië."

Zody laughed. "Are you any good with it?"

"Well, no but—"

Tristan held out his hand. "Let me take the crossbow," he said. "You stay here with Zody."

Clovis hesitated. Then he held the weapon close to his chest. "No," he said. "I want to fight."

"Fine. I'll go with you," Tristan said, following Kaië and Clovis down the hill. Zody stood at the mouth of the tunnel, astounded at Tristan's audacity.

"What are you doing?" he shouted. "I told you, you don't have a weapon!"

"I'll find one!" Tristan called back.

Zody paced back and forth in the tunnel. If he stayed, he'd be safe. But what if everyone else died and no one knew where to find him? If he went with Tristan, he'd get killed for sure, but then again, maybe not. He juggled these thoughts for several moments. Finally he made a decision. "Wait up! I'm coming with you!" he said and then added under his breath, "I really hate dragons!"

Fifty-four

The door at the top of the tower stairs creaked as Marcus pushed it open. He stepped into a bare round room with a wooden floor. To his right, a window opened to the sea. To his left, a rope ladder hung against the wall, leading to a framework of rafters above. Arik stood in the center of the room, his hair disheveled, his cloak torn. A gash on his upper arm bled profusely. His cloak concealed his other arm.

"You've arrived in the nick of time," he said, his lips thinning into a cynical grin. "A moment later and I may very well have done something I might regret."

Arik pulled his cloak away. Beneath it, clasped in the bend of his elbow, was Kelvin. Arik held him around the neck so that he could not speak and struggled to breathe.

"Let him go!" shouted Marcus through clenched teeth. Anger burned within him. "I said let him go!"

Arik laughed.

"You are fierce for one so young," he said. "I suppose you want to kill me. It won't matter if you do. If you look out that window there, you will see the fleet of Dokur in ruins, while my men row to shore in skiffs I designed to withstand the treacherous tides of Imaness. And even if they are unsuccessful, my dragons—trained for war from the time they were hatchlings—cannot be defeated. So kill me if you like, but Dokur is doomed."

The sight of Dokur's incinerated navy and the countless skiffs carrying enemy soldiers rowing across the harbor struck Marcus through his very heart. The enemy seemed numberless. Jayson would never arrive in time.

"I know who you are!" said Marcus. "I know how you betrayed Jayson and Ivanore. And now you betray your own father!"

Arik laughed menacingly. "Is that what Jayson told you? Did he tell you of his own treachery? How he broke the law by marrying my sister? Did he tell you how I got *this*?"

Arik turned his face aside, and Marcus winced at the sight of the ugly, pulsating scar.

"You've won, Arik," said Marcus. "Dokur is as good as fallen. As for Kelvin, you don't need him. Release him, and I vow to leave you in peace."

"Release him? *Release him?*" Arik tightened his grip on Kelvin's neck. "This *child* has wounded me with this pitiful little dagger," he said, holding Kelvin's dagger in his hand. "I was just about to break his neck when you so rudely interrupted me."

Marcus didn't think. Roaring with rage, he plunged forward with his sword pointed straight ahead of him. Arik warded the attack by twisting his body to the left and flinging Marcus aside. Though his initial attack failed, Marcus's sudden advance distracted Arik long enough for Kelvin to break free. Seeing that he was now outnumbered, Arik scurried up the rope ladder and disappeared into the web of timbers above.

Kelvin knelt on the floor, rubbing his throat with his hands. "Will you go after him or shall I?" he croaked, but Marcus had already leapt off the top rung and into the rafters.

The uppermost area of the tower was bathed in shadow. A cone-shaped slate roof rose high overhead, letting in no light. The only illumination ascended through the crisscross of beams, creating an eerie illusion of layered shadows.

Marcus balanced on a twelve-inch beam that spanned the width of the room below. More beams crossed above his head, supporting the roof. One beam sloped low enough for him to grab hold of and steady himself as he inched his way across. Somewhere, in one of the deep pockets of blackness, Arik waited for him.

The air was stifling. Marcus's skin tingled, and the moisture that formed on his body dampened his clothes. The cramped darkness filled him with dread, and though he struggled to keep his memories in check, images from his dreams flooded his mind. Once again he heard the warboar of his childhood breathing in his ears. He closed his eyes for a moment, fighting back the fear that threatened to overwhelm him.

Marcus opened his eyes wide and scanned the darkness for signs of movement. He wiped the sweat from his brow and took a deep breath to calm himself. His lungs burned from the suffocating dust that blurred the air like a haze. The sound of air rushing in and out of them seemed as loud as the waves crashing against the shore outside. In and out, the rhythm steady as a drum. In and out. In and out. Marcus caught his breath and held it, yet the rhythm of someone else's breathing echoed in his ears.

Marcus spun around, and his blade clashed against Arik's dagger, halting a deadly blow from behind. The force of the blow knocked Marcus off balance. He fell, grasping the beam with his arms as his sword clattered to the floor below.

"What a predicament!" said Arik, amused. "I suppose you expect me to toy with you now, or to do the gentlemanly thing and pull you up so we can continue this farce." He placed the toe of his boot over Marcus's fingers. A sharp pain shot through his hand and he screamed out. "I hate to disappoint you," continued Arik, "but I don't like playing games."

Arik raised the dagger, point down, above Marcus's head. Suddenly Arik shot forward, as though some abrupt force had collided with him from behind. His face smashed into the beam as he fell. Holding onto him was Kelvin. The two of them hit the floor below with a sickening thud. And then there was silence mingled with the sounds of the sea crashing against the cliffs below.

Fifty-five

arcus swung his leg over the rafter and pulled himself up. He made his way as quickly as safety would allow to the ladder and hurried down it. He ran to the tangled mass that was Arik and Kelvin. Arik lay unconscious. Kelvin was alive, though his breathing was sporadic and labored.

"Kelvin, are you all right?" asked Marcus, tenderly pressing here and there on Kelvin's body to assess the damage.

"It's hard to breathe," Kelvin whispered.

"You've broken some ribs." Marcus tried to sound encouraging. "I'll bind them for you. In a few weeks you'll be as good as new."

"No." Kelvin's voice was weak but resolute. "I'm not going to make it, Marcus."

"I'll find a doctor."

"There isn't time." Kelvin wheezed. Blood trickled from the corner of his mouth. His body convulsed, and Marcus's throat went dry.

"I'll hurry," said Marcus, steadying the waver in his voice.

Kelvin shook his head. "I don't want to die in here."

Marcus needed help. He quickly gathered up his sword and sheathed it. Xerxes immediately came to life.

"What's happened?" he asked, seeing Kelvin and Arik lying on the floor.

"Kelvin is injured," Marcus explained as he tried to lift his friend. "I've got to help him, but without the key, what can I do?"

For the first time, Xerxes had no words to offer. He looked at Marcus with empathy. "You will find a way. I have confidence in you," he said and then went silent.

Marcus did not know the source of the strength that sprang up within him, but as he bore the weight of Kelvin's body on his back, he knew that if necessary, he could carry him all the way to Quendel.

The sun had begun its gradual descent by the time they stepped out of the tower. In the slowly fading light of day, the fate of Dokur was clear. The boats had landed. The enemy had come ashore.

Fifty-six

Hestoria's flag was already planted on the shore when Marcus emerged from the watchtower. The dragon's black wing on a background of blue flapped wildly in the wind. The air swarmed with dragons heaving breaths of fire on the remains of the crippled navy. Russet-skinned Hestorian soldiers, hundreds of them, were gathered in battalions along the beach below the Fortress. Hundreds more still waited offshore in their boats. Each of them held a diamond-shaped shield in one hand and a short, curved scimitar in the other. In their glinting armor, which covered their chests, arms, backs, and heads, they seemed invincible.

With Kelvin's now-unconscious body slung across his back, Marcus slipped behind the tower and made his way up the steep hill to the far wall of the Fortress. His progress was slow, however, as Kelvin was taller and broader than he, and Marcus had to stop frequently to shift Kelvin's weight to his shoulders. When the burden became almost unbearable, he would again let Kelvin slide a few inches down his back. After only a few minutes, a sharp pain radiated from the base of Marcus's neck all the way down to his ankles. But he ignored it and continued placing one foot in front of the other. After what seemed like hours, he felt the ground level off beneath his feet. He was on the far side of the Fortress. On the other side was the hill and the secret tunnel. Beyond that was Dokur.

Making his way through a dense row of trees, Marcus soon found himself at the edge of a clearing. He laid Kelvin beneath one of the trees. Kelvin was breathing, but his face was pale.

"I don't know what to do," Marcus told him, even though Kelvin hadn't moved or spoken since they left the tower. "I have to go for help."

Marcus removed his cape and tucked it over his friend, making sure that he was warm and well hidden. Then, drawing his sword once more and leaving Xerxes' empty sheath beside Kelvin, he struck out for Dokur.

Doing his best to keep out of the dragons' sight, he made his way around the southern gate. The guards that had been there earlier were nowhere to be found. He imagined Lord Fredric had gathered what forces he could to hold off the Hestorians until the Agorans arrived.

He was now only a short distance from the city. The sounds of screams filled his ears. When he reached the outskirts, he ducked behind a washhouse. Dokur was in chaos. Hundreds of citizens fled their homes, crowding the one road leading out of the city, while Hestorian soldiers picked them off like flies. Others hid in their homes, only to be rooted out at sword point. In the center of the town square, dozens of captive citizens huddled in a single mass surrounded by enemy soldiers. Men stood around the perimeter, while the women and children clustered together in the center. Except for the occasional cry of a young child, these people were silent, defiant, and proud.

The Hestorian soldiers brandished their scimitars at the terrified captives. While Marcus watched, the soldiers parted, and a burly-looking captain strutted forward.

"I am General Tark!" he said, his voice booming like thunder. "I am your new sovereign! Any of you who wishes to live will bow down to me and pledge your loyalty."

Not a single soul moved from his place. The soldiers tensed their sinewy arms and readied for the kill.

General Tark stepped toward the group of captives and grabbed a young man by the hair, dragging him from the embrace of an older woman whom Marcus supposed was his mother. The general forced the man to his knees. The man winced in pain but uttered not a word.

"Bow to me!"

The young man did not bow. Instead he spat in Tark's face. The general lifted his scimitar and swung it like a sickle across the man's abdomen. At first Marcus wondered whether the blade had actually come in contact with the man's body at all, but then as if in slow motion, he fell forward, the top half of his body separating from the bottom half as he struck the ground. The man's mother screamed and then collapsed to the ground, sobbing.

General Tark raised his right arm, preparing to give the signal of attack to his men. The sounds of children whimpering and of women praying rose up from the crowd.

If only I had the key, Marcus thought to himself. I could destroy the enemy with an earthquake or hurricane! Such thoughts were not comforting, however, since he knew he did not possess the strength necessary to perform such miracles, and even if he did, the key was lost.

"I'm sorry, Kelvin," whispered Marcus, tears forming against his will. "If you die, it will be because I have died as well, but I can't watch this merciless slaughter and do nothing."

He felt the weight of the blade in his hand. Despite his original dislike for Xerxes, the enchanted staff and sword had served him well. He hoped that when he lay dead, Jayson would find him and take Xerxes as his own. He thought of Zyll and hoped someone would bring him word of his death, perhaps one of the other boys. He had not seen Clovis and the others since before entering the watchtower, nor had he seen Kaië. He hoped they had escaped.

The Hestorian soldiers pressed closer to the frightened group of townsfolk. By the sneers on their faces. they seemed to enjoy this game of taunting them with death. The thought of anyone taking pleasure in the suffering of others angered Marcus. He tightened his grip on his sword and rose from his hiding place. But as he was about to dive into the mass of soldiers he heard what he thought was a horn sounding. The soldiers heard it, too, as did the townspeople. They stopped to listen.

The horn sounded again, louder than before. When it sounded the third time, the shouts of hundreds of men split the air. The Agoran slave army poured through the streets like living water, running and beating their chests as though they had already won the battle.

Fifty-seven

The Hestorians were so stunned by the sudden appearance of the Agoran army that they stood motionless as the slaves descended upon them. But their shock was only momentary. They began swinging their weapons with the ferocity of caged lions. Soon bodies were piled high, and blood flowed in the streets. The Agorans had no armor and were vulnerable to the bite of the Hestorian blades, but nothing could match their will and resolve, for unlike the Hestorians who fought for wealth and greed, the Agorans fought for freedom.

Marcus ran into the midst of the fray, his sword slashing at the first Hestorian in his path and then another. He did not fear for his own life but wanted to reach the center of the marketplace where the unarmed citizens of Dokur still stood, now trapped by the fighting around them. Marcus reached the outer circle of men and saw a look of longing and desperation in their eyes.

"Do you have any weapons?" shouted Marcus above the din of clashing metal.

"We have," said one man, "but we had no time to retrieve them before we were rounded up like animals to slaughter."

"I will lead your families to safety," continued Marcus. "Then you can get your weapons and return to defend your city."

The men nodded and then turned to explain the plan to their families. There was no time to debate its plausibility, for if they stayed where they were, they would all be killed.

Marcus made his way through a group of Hestorians, injuring two along the way. The men of Dokur formed a tight layer of defense around their women and children and moved as quickly as possible through the passage Marcus had made for them. More than one man took a blow from an enemy, but by the time they reached the grassy knoll below the Fortress, though many had been injured, not one life had been lost.

Marcus spoke to the men once again. "I will lead your families to the far side of the Fortress. They'll be safe there. Go now and fetch your weapons—anything! Your Agoran brothers need your help."

Marcus led the women and children down the same path he had previously taken, where the refugees were well out of their enemy's view. He accompanied them as far as the Fortress gate and then stopped. "It's getting dark, but if you continue on the path around the Fortress you will reach a clearing bordered with trees. Wait there. Do not pass through the trees, or the ships may spot you from the harbor."

He watched, satisfied, as the procession continued without him. Just as the last families were passing by, he saw the woman whose son had been killed by the Hestorian general. She carried with her a large cloth bag. He called to her and the woman approached him. "You are the Liberator," she said in a hushed tone.

Marcus shook his head. "No," he said, "the man you seek is down there in the battle."

"I should like to thank him," she continued.

"If he survives, if anyone of us survives, I will see to it that you meet him. Are you a doctor?" asked Marcus, indicating the bag in her hand.

"Nay," said the woman, "I am a midwife."

Marcus's disappointment must have shown on his face, for the woman opened her bag and showed him its contents: herbs of all kinds and a few rudimentary medical tools.

"However," she continued, "on occasion I am called upon to aid those who fall ill. You might say I dabble in the art of herbal healing."

Relieved that his instinct had been correct after all, Marcus told the woman about Kelvin and gave her directions to find him. He hoped she might be of assistance until a true doctor could be found.

Marcus looked up and saw what appeared to be a black cloud above the harbor. With the destruction of Dokur's ships complete, the horde of enemy dragons now headed toward the city. Turning back, Marcus ran as fast as he could to the battlefield.

Fifty-eight

"We'll take weapons from the dead," said Tristan, scanning the town square from a safe distance behind the tavern. Kaië had led him there along with Zody and Clovis in hopes of finding swords for them, but the locker that normally housed the tavern's collection of them was empty. As they watched the battle raging, they knew they must either return to safety or somehow obtain new weapons.

"We won't make it!" said Zody. "We'll get run through for sure!"

"Let *me* go." Kaië was adamant. "They might think twice about striking down a woman." Zody was about to agree with her, when a startling sight stopped them both.

Tristan was already halfway to the square, weaving through the combatants.

"Look at him!" said Zody.

Staying low to the ground, Tristan soon reached the square. He knelt beside a fallen Hestorian and pried the bloody scimitar from his hand. He turned toward his friends and gleefully waved the weapon over his head. A moment later, another Hestorian stepped in front of him, scimitar raised and ready to attack. But the soldier never swung his weapon. Instead he froze where he stood, a look of agony on his face. Then he crumpled to the ground, dead with a single arrow in his back. Behind him stood Clovis, crossbow raised and discharged.

"Great shot!" shouted Zody, slapping Clovis on the back. Clovis smiled weakly, but his smile quickly disappeared.

"What's the matter?" asked Zody. "You look pale. You're not going to faint, are you?"

Clovis lifted a shaky finger and pointed above Zody's head. Zody slowly turned and found himself eye to eye with a hideous dragon. The beast reared back and beat its wings, which spanned the entire length of the tavern. Its black scales glistened like oil, and smoke streamed from the corners of its mouth, which was large enough to bite a man in two.

"Run!" shouted Kaië, grabbing Clovis by the collar and racing toward the square. Zody tried to follow, but the sensation of the dragon's hot breath on his skin made his legs feel like rubber.

Kaië reached Tristan and called over her shoulder. "Come on, Zody!"

The dragon leapt onto the tavern's roof. It blew columns of fire from its nostrils, setting the neighboring building aflame. The wooden structure lit up like a bonfire, eerily illuminating the battle in the fading daylight. Mustering every ounce of strength he could, Zody ran toward Kaië.

"Quick! Find me a sword!" he said and then muttered, "I really, *really* hate dragons."

Fifty-nine

By the time Marcus returned to the marketplace, the battle between the Agorans and the Hestorians was in full sway. The men of Dokur had taken up arms and joined in the fight. But Marcus was dismayed to see how well the enemy's armor protected them, while every blow to an Agoran left him wounded or dead. As the sun continued its descent into the sea, Marcus feared certain defeat. And to make matters worse, the dragons were setting whole sections of the town on fire.

A feeling of despair settled on Marcus, but the sight of a familiar face quickly restored his hope. Jayson, his clothes torn and bloody, valiantly fought off three Hestorian soldiers. Spinning to his right, he dispatched the first with his sword and then buried his blade into another's stomach. The third met his fate when his head was separated from his neck.

Marcus waved his sword over his head. "Jayson! Jayson, it's me, Marcus!" he shouted. At that moment, a sharp pain tore through Marcus's right shoulder. Then the cold point of a dagger was pressed against his throat. A hoarse voice whispered in his ear.

"So we meet again, Marcus!"

Arik! A terrible dread filled Marcus as he realized that the blood dripping from the blade at his throat was his own, and the pain in his shoulder was from the wound it had left behind. Arik wrenched the sword from Marcus's hand and threw it aside, then pressed the dagger deeper into his esophagus.

"Jayson!" shouted Arik. "I have the boy!"

Jayson finished off two more Hestorians and then advanced toward Arik. His eyes were set like steel, but Arik pulled back on Marcus's shoulder. Marcus screamed out in pain. Jayson stopped abruptly.

"Let him go!" demanded Jayson. "The boy means nothing to you!"

"Nothing? He killed my Mardoks and nearly killed me! For that reason alone I would take great pleasure in disemboweling him. Yet seeing how you've taken quite a fancy to each other, as long as he lives," Arik snarled, "I have some influence over *you*!"

Jayson's expression revealed no emotion. His jaw was set and his eyes were fixed on Arik. He said nothing but took one threatening step toward his enemy.

Arik shouted like a rabid animal. "I will kill him! I swear it!"

"What do you want from me, Arik?"

"Only what is rightfully mine! Imaness is home to the only known deposit of Celestine. Once I possess it, I will control the rarest and costliest treasure in this part of the world."

"Even if you do take the Celestine, who will mine it for you?" said Jayson. "The Agorans are no longer slaves. They fight for their freedom even now."

"Call them back!" demanded Arik. "Stop this battle and command your slaves back to the mines, or I will drench the ground with this boy's blood!"

"I can't let you take the mine."

Arik's grip on Marcus tightened. "I would have shared my riches with you, but you betrayed me!"

"*I* betrayed *you?*" said Jayson, his eyes burning with both grief and rage. "You robbed me of the only possession that has any value to me at all. I know the truth, Arik! You betrayed your own sister! It is because of you that she is gone!"

Jayson took the parchment scroll from beneath his cloak and tossed it on the ground at Arik's feet. "Take it, then, if paper, ink, and jewels mean so much to you. And take this as well!"

He reached into his leather pouch and held up a dry, shriveled human ear. "Do you remember how you lost it, Arik? Do you remember how I severed it from your head with this very blade? Let the boy go, or I will have no choice but to do the same to the rest of you," said Jayson, throwing the ear down beside the map.

Arik's very frame trembled from anger, the hatred in him surging like a tempest. Marcus's head grew light. He wanted to vomit. The pain in his shoulder throbbed, and he felt the warmth of his blood oozing down his back. He tried to keep his eyes focused, but the scene before him melted into a blur of color and shadow. Then there was only darkness.

Sixty

Arik teetered off balance as Marcus's limp body fell against him. In that split second, Jayson was upon him. He attacked Arik with a barrage of powerful blows, wounding him in the arm and chest. Arik shoved Marcus aside and ran, snatching a sword from a fallen soldier as he went.

Jayson pursued Arik, and their conflict continued across the town square toward the perimeter of Dokur. Each man, spurred on by his hatred of the other, struggled to get the upper hand. As they neared the edge of the plateau above the road, Arik began to show signs of weakness. Finally, his energy spent, Arik dropped to his knees and threw his sword over the cliff.

"I concede," he said, his chest heaving. "I am mortally wounded. Let me die with what dignity I have remaining."

Jayson thrust the point of his sword against Arik's abdomen. "Dignity? What dignity is there in plotting to invade your own homeland and to slaughter your own people?"

"My father's people!" said Arik, the words spewing from his mouth like venom. "Dokur's beloved Fredric is content to squander my inheritance! I was his heir until Ivanore bore a son. As a woman, Ivanore could never rule. But her son! Yes, I betrayed you. My jealousy drove me to it. I thought I would gain my father's favor. How was I to know that Fredric would kill the child?"

Arik raised his hands to his face as if to hide from the shame he felt. "I tried to stop him," he continued, his voice breaking. "But in his rage, he exiled me and stripped me of my inheritance."

Jayson's heart ached inside him. The anger that had consumed him moments before turned to compassion. "The child is not dead," he said, lowering his sword. "Ivanore took him away. I don't know where he is now, but I believe he is alive. Come with me and make amends with your father."

The effort was painful, but Arik rose to one knee. As Jayson reached out his hand to help him, a single arrow suddenly pierced Arik's chest. He collapsed into Jayson's arms. Jayson turned to identify the culprit but saw only the crowd of battling soldiers.

Jayson looked back at Arik, whose breath now came in short, painful snatches. "Do you think . . . Fredric . . . " Arik's words were broken as his body convulsed. He struggled to continue. "Will my father . . . forgive me?"

Jayson nodded. He tried to utter the words he felt in his heart, but the tightness in his throat and chest prevented him from speaking. He nodded again, and Arik smiled slightly. As the life ebbed out of him, Arik's eyes flickered and then shut forever.

*   *   *

The arrows in Clovis's quiver were nearly gone. With them he had wounded seven Hestorian soldiers. Tristan had wounded four with his sword and received two shallow wounds of his own. They had found shelter behind the city's fountain while Kaië saw to Tristan's injuries.

Zody knelt beside Tristan, offering words of encouragement. "Can't be all that bad," he said. "They're just flesh wounds. Your arm will heal soon enough."

"Easy for you to say!" snapped Tristan, clenching his teeth while Kaië tied a strip of cloth just above his elbow. "You've managed quite well to stay clear of danger."

"I was never very good with a sword," said Zody, examining the clean blade he held in his hand.

Just then Clovis cried out. "Look over there! It's Jayson and Arik!"

He pointed toward the entrance to the city, where Jayson stood holding a sword to Arik's chest. To their

astonishment, however, Jayson did not kill Arik but lowered his sword, offering his hand to help the other man
up. Suddenly, mere yards from where the boys sat watching, a lone archer turned and fired an arrow straight
through Arik's heart.

"Did you see that?" said Clovis. "That guard just
killed Arik!"

"He had it coming," said Zody.

Before Jayson could even turn around, the archer
drew another arrow, aiming it right at Jayson's back.

"He's going to kill Jayson!" shouted Clovis.

"Clovis, your bow!" said Tristan.

Clovis began wheezing heavily. "I've only got one
arrow left—and it's broken!"

Kaië grabbed Zody by his shirtsleeve and pulled him
to his feet. "Go!" she told him. "You're the only one with
a sword in your hand, so go! Go now!"

Zody leapt to his feet and threw himself across the
space that separated him from Jayson's attacker. There
wasn't a moment to hesitate or to think. In half a second,
Zody's sword came down on the archer's forearm. The
man screamed out in pain as his arrow shot wide. The
culprit turned and ran, blending into the crowd of battling soldiers.

Another second later, Zody once again dropped down
beside Tristan, gasping for breath. Kaië squeezed his
hand. Clovis patted him on the shoulder.

"I did it! I can't believe I actually did it," said Zody,
smiling proudly at his companions. "You know, saving

someone's life feels pretty good. I'll have to try it again
sometime."

* * *

Jayson rose from Arik's lifeless body and turned back
toward Dokur. The scene before him filled him with sorrow, for many of his Agoran brethren lay wounded on the
battlefield, far more than the number of Hestorians. The
dragons, not content to set buildings and ships ablaze,
had taken to scavenging upon the bodies of the dead and
dying. It was a gruesome sight. Though the war waged
on, Jayson could see the fear and desperation in the
Agorans' eyes.

Not far off, Nathar, the Agoran slave, was engaged in
combat with a heavily armored enemy. Wounded and
weak, Nathar barely had strength to withstand the blows.
Jayson ran to his aid, but he was too late. With one last
strike, the Hestorian gained the final victory. Within
moments a hungry dragon lumbered across the battlefield, its bloodstained talons leaving gaping holes in the
earth as it came. From the depths of Jayson's soul, a roar
erupted. He ran toward his fallen comrade and threw himself before the beast.

"Get away!" he shouted with inhuman fury. "Get
away from him!"

The dragon reared its head, unleashing a spray of
sparks that fell around the Agoran warrior like an umbrella
of fire. Jayson sprinted forward and lodged his sword in

the beast's throat. The dragon screeched in pain and then slashed at its attacker with a full set of razor-sharp talons. Jayson managed to jump free from the blow, but without a weapon, he was no match for the wounded dragon. The dragon beat its wings furiously as it worked the sword loose from its own throat and then crushed it between its massive teeth. It started toward Jayson, but then the dragon screeched again. A large tear appeared in its right wing. The glint of a sword slashed through the air and another tear appeared. The dragon tucked its wounded wing beneath its body. Behind it, Marcus held Xerxes' blade in a feeble grip.

As the dragon retreated, Marcus's legs buckled beneath him. Jayson ran forward and caught him as he fell. He set Marcus gently on the ground and covered him with his cloak.

"Despite all my efforts to free my people," said Jayson as tears threatened to fall, "I have instead led them straight to hell. Maybe it would have been better to live as slaves than to die like this."

Marcus shivered and drew up Jayson's cloak to his chin. "You're wrong," he said. "Some things are worth dying for."

Jayson was about to reply, but he realized that Marcus had once again slipped into unconsciousness. He turned again to Nathar. To his relief, the wounded Agoran was breathing. It was then that Jayson noticed what was clutched in Nathar's fingers: the banner bearing Fredric's royal seal. Though soiled and torn, the words he had written there were still legible. He carefully pulled the fabric free. Then he strode across the battlefield to the great fountain at the town center. Climbing to the highest point he could reach, he took up the banner and raised it above his head, shouting for all to hear. "For our families, our land, and our liberty!"

On hearing Jayson's words and seeing the banner raised, the Agorans' determination was renewed. Though they might all die that day, it would be for a just cause. They would die for those things most dear to them. Theirs would be a worthy sacrifice, indeed.

The ground beneath Jayson's feet began to tremble. Thunder sounded, or something that sounded like thunder. In reality it was the sound of giant footsteps. Jayson hurried to the edge of the plateau and saw more than a dozen Cyclopes running across the valley. Once they reached the road leading to the city, they ascended it in a matter of seconds. Without hesitation, they joined the Agorans in battle.

When Breah saw Jayson, he bent down for his customary rub behind the ears. Vos stood nearby, as well.

"Are we too late?" Vos asked.

"You're just in time," replied Jayson. "But how did you know to come? At the lake I dared not ask you to fight."

"Let us say a boy who didn't want to become my supper said you might be in trouble."

"Your supper? But Cyclopes are vegetarians."

"Yes," replied Vos, laughing. "But the boy didn't know that."

At the sight of the giants, both the Agorans and Hestorians were equally petrified with fear. But seeing one of the Cyclopes lift Jayson to its shoulder gave the Agorans a surge of courage. The Cyclopes moved through the armies, picking out the Hestorians as though they were mere insects and flinging them into the sea. The dragons were swatted down like flies. Those that managed to escape the Cyclopes' hands ran for the harbor. Soon the remaining enemy soldiers had all fled toward the shore. They could not board their boats fast enough. Those skiffs that got away in time managed to reach the safety of their ships. The others were capsized like toys in a child's bath, their occupants thrown well out of the harbor and left to swim for it.

The battle of Dokur was over.

Sixty-one

By the time Marcus regained consciousness, the Hestorians had deserted Dokur. Jayson held a cup of water to Marcus's parched lips, and he drank it gratefully. He tried to sit up, but the pain in his shoulder was immense.

"That's Arik's handiwork you feel," said Jayson, cradling Marcus's head in his hands. "It's not as bad as it seems. A minor wound, but painful. I'll take you to an inn where you can rest."

"No," protested Marcus weakly. "I must—" His voice broke off, and he winced from the pain. "I must get to Kelvin. He needs a doctor."

The look on Jayson's face did nothing to alleviate Marcus's concern.

"I'm sorry, Marcus, but there's only one physician in Dokur, and he is overwhelmed with seeing to the soldiers. I cannot ask him . . . "

Jayson averted his eyes from Marcus and hung his head. Marcus struggled to sit up and fought even harder to stand. He looked around him. The devastation that lay before him was far more than he could have imagined. Though the Cyclopes had managed to rid Dokur of its enemy, many of the buildings were nothing but blackened rubble. The glow from a few scattered fires cast shifting shadows among the dead. The stench of blood and ash filled the air.

Only one image stood out among the rest as a beacon of hope: Fredric's banner hoisted high on a makeshift pole. The words written there reassured Marcus that all would be well.

"I must go to Kelvin," Marcus said. He took a step forward, but his legs gave way beneath him. Jayson caught him by the arm to steady him. Then, finding Marcus's sword on the ground nearby, he placed it in the boy's hand. Marcus wrapped his grip around Xerxes and felt the comfort of his old companion. Leaning his weight against the sword, he took another step. He would have taken one more, but Jayson stepped in front of him, blocking his path.

"Wait," he said, "I'll go with you."

*   *   *

Darkness had settled on Dokur like a shroud. As the large fires were put out by trains of people with buckets, torches dotted the village, casting dancing phantoms against the buildings. The pile of bodies in the center of the marketplace grew to the height of the rooftops—and yet there were still more. On the morrow, they would be burned in a ceremonial pyre.

Marcus leaned heavily on Xerxes as he led Jayson around the outer gate of the Fortress. With only a single torch to light their way, their path was more treacherous than it had been in daylight, making the journey much longer than Marcus would have preferred. Once the full moon rose overhead, however, the trail, illuminated by its silver glow, became easier to follow.

Just when Marcus could stand the waiting no longer, the column of trees appeared before him in the distance. Nothing could hold him back now, and though he had not yet regained his full strength, he ran across the field, stumbling only once along the way.

The children of Dokur were nestled quietly in their mothers' laps beneath the canopy of green. The wind rustling through the leaves played a comforting lullaby. Jayson stopped to speak to the wives of those men who had fought so valiantly. Marcus continued on and finally found the old midwife hunched over Kelvin and applying a layer of ointment over his wounds.

"Your friend is not well," she told him. "I have done all I can, but I fear it is not enough."

Marcus knelt on the ground beside Kelvin and placed a hand on his cheek. Kelvin's skin was moist and hot to the touch. His breath was shallow and irregular. At Marcus's touch, Kelvin's eyelids opened. His gaze wandered at first, but finally settled on Marcus's face. "I'm glad you're here," whispered Kelvin. Forming the words was a struggle. "Take this." With great effort he removed the Celestine pendant from around his neck and placed it in Marcus's hand.

"I can't take it," said Marcus, fighting back tears. Kelvin looked as though he wanted to say more, but his eyes rolled back in his head, and he slipped back into unconsciousness.

"Will he . . . ?" Marcus began, though he could not finish the sentence.

The midwife looked at him with a mother's concern. "He will not live through the night," she said.

"But there must be something more we can do!"

The midwife shook her head. "I'm sorry."

For a fleeting moment, Marcus thought of Zyll's key. With its power there must surely be some way to help, but it was gone—and with it all hope of saving Kelvin. Then a thought struck him.

He found the staff where he had left it and sheathed his sword. When he rapped on Xerxes' beak, the bird fluttered to life. "What do you mean, striking me that way?" he squawked irritably. "I've a good mind to mention this in my report to Zyll."

"Don't be angry, Xerxes," said Marcus. "I need you to

tell me something about the key. Is it possible to do magic without it? Zyll doesn't use any charm."

Xerxes ground his beak together while contemplating his answer. "That depends," he replied finally.

"Depends on what?" asked Marcus.

"On you, of course," answered Xerxes. "You *are* an enchanter-in-training, you know. Did you think you would need the key forever?"

"Then I can perform magic on my own!" Marcus turned to Kelvin, whose pale face had the look of impending death upon it. "But how can I heal Kelvin when the magic only works on inorganic materials?"

"Where did you hear that nonsense?" replied Xerxes.

"I heard it from you," said Marcus. "You said it was impossible to manipulate organic objects, that not even Zyll could do it."

"I said it was *nearly* impossible, which is entirely different."

"Then it can be done!"

Marcus grasped Kelvin's shirt in his hands and tore open the fabric, revealing his bruised and broken body. As he laid his hands on Kelvin's chest, Xerxes squawked in protest.

"Wait! I know how much you care for Kelvin. I've grown to tolerate him, as well. But you mustn't use your powers this way! You've seen how magic drains you of energy. Transmuting an organic substance, especially someone on death's door, would virtually require your life force in exchange for his!"

"What are you saying, Xerxes?"

"I'm saying you're not strong enough. Few enchanters are! Even the mighty Zyll will not take such risks. And you are only an apprentice!"

Marcus knew that Xerxes was right—he had felt weakened each time he used magic—but he could not bear to watch Kelvin die. "I have no choice," he said. "I must try to save him."

With his palms against Kelvin's chest, Marcus imagined in his mind how he could manipulate bone and flesh to mend itself. He tried to think what command he should use, but then Kelvin's body shuddered. His breath went out of him and his heart ceased beating.

The midwife began to weep. By now Jayson had joined Marcus by Kelvin's side. He placed a comforting hand on Marcus's shoulder.

"He's gone," he said.

Marcus leaned over Kelvin and enfolded the lifeless body of his friend in his arms. The tears began slowly at first, then came faster. Marcus's body shook, and he wept from more grief than he had ever known. As he wept, however, his grief turned to anger, the anger to rage.

"No! I won't let you die! You must live!" he shouted, his voice erupting in uncontrollable sobs. "Live! Do you hear me? I command it! Live! Live! LIVE!"

The night was silent except for the intermittent sounds of children whimpering in their mothers' arms as they slept. Jayson, the midwife, and a few women from Dokur stood by watching the anguished boy mourn the death of his friend. So quiet were they that when Kelvin took that first deep breath, they all heard it and were astonished. After the second breath, the midwife quickly fell to her knees beside him and felt his pulse.

"His heart is beating!" she said. A quick examination of his chest found clean, new skin and solid bone where only wounds had been before. She clasped her hands together and praised the gods for the miracle. Only then did she notice the other boy on the ground, his body crumpled and unmoving.

Sixty-two

Marcus opened his eyes and blinked against the bright light. While his eyes adjusted he tried to make out his surroundings. He was lying prone on the ground underneath a tall tree, the same tree beneath which he had knelt beside Kelvin. But Kelvin was gone. Everyone was gone.

He stood up. His legs felt surprisingly strong. Everything looked the same: the trees, the meadow, the Fortress, even the sound of waves crashing on the shore. Yet it wasn't the same, not quite.

He called out. "Hello?" His voice sounded distant, as if it were someone else's voice. "Where is everyone?"

Even before he saw her, he knew he wasn't alone. He turned and there she was, standing right beside him, her long, flaxen hair billowing in the breeze. She was a stranger to him, yet somehow familiar.

"Are you my angel?" he asked. The woman smiled at him, but her eyes betrayed a profound sadness. She lifted her arm and unfolded the fingers of her hand, bidding Marcus to take the object that lay there. As he did so, he immediately recognized its triangular shape and blue-green hue.

"Kelvin's pendant?" He was puzzled. "Why are you giving me this?" But the woman did not answer. Her form faded into a soft white mist that rose above the meadow and floated away over the treetops. As Marcus watched her go, he raised his hand to shield his eyes from the blinding light.

* * *

Morning broke with the sun peeking through the cluster of tree trunks, spilling golden beams on the faces of those who slept. Marcus stirred and listened to the chorus of birds calling to one another and to the rhythmic crash of high tide. Although he still felt physically weak from the night before, his energy of spirit had returned.

Nearby, Jayson stoked a fire around which several children had gathered to warm themselves. The flames' brilliant glow seemed harsh against the softer light of daybreak.

"Well, well! He's not dead after all," said Jayson, grinning.

"Good morning to you, too," Marcus replied, yawning. The memory of the previous night's events came back to him like a tidal wave.

"Kelvin . . . " he began anxiously.

"He's sleeping soundly." Jayson nodded toward the young man curled up on the earth beside the nearest tree. "You never told me you could perform miracles."

"He's all right?"

"Not a scratch. Just worn out. Both of you. You didn't move an inch all night. For a while, I thought you were dead."

Marcus laughed a little. "So did I," he said. As he tried to stand, a sharp pain shot through him, and he nearly collapsed. Jayson hurried to his side and offered his arm for Marcus to lean on.

"You should rest. That wound in your shoulder needs time to heal."

"I'm fine, really," answered Marcus, wincing as he stood. "Just a little stiff, that's all."

Jayson helped Marcus to the campfire, where he sat among a circle of children who were finishing their breakfasts. On seeing the one who saved them, they gathered around him, clinging to his arms and legs and bestowing upon him endless hugs and kisses. Marcus laughed with delight.

"All right, all right," he said. "Back to your mothers now. We'll be returning to the village soon."

Marcus felt impatient to share his dream of the night before with Jayson and was glad when they were finally alone. He described every detail of what he had seen: of the light, the angel, and her gift to him. He also told of how he had hidden himself in Fredric's council chambers and what he had seen there.

"I saw your crystal, the one Ivanore gave you, and I knew I had seen it before." Holding Kelvin's pendant out to Jayson, he went on. "I think you should have this."

Jayson took the pendant in his hand. "This is part of Ivanore's royal seal," he said, brushing his fingers over its surface. "Where did you get this?"

Marcus hesitated to respond. He sensed from Jayson's voice that this shard of Celestine had renewed a failing hope within him. He knew how far Jayson had come to find his family, and he feared the answer would be more than he could bear. However, Marcus could only speak the truth. "It belongs to Kelvin," he said. "His mother gave it to him—before she died."

Jayson's expression changed to one of bewilderment, then to shock, and finally to grief. "She really is gone then," he said, his eyes betraying the sorrow within him. Rising to his feet, he walked to the trees, pausing briefly to gaze on Kelvin's sleeping form. Then, continuing on, he slipped into the grove and disappeared from sight.

Sixty-three

Marcus laid another log on the fire. As the flames consumed the new wood, he noticed movement near the Fortress. Placing his hand on the hilt of his sword, he called out, "Who's there?" But to his surprise and relief, three familiar faces appeared. Tristan waved his arms and came running, with Zody and Clovis following close behind.

"Marcus, you're all right!" said Tristan.

Marcus embraced his friends and invited them to sit down beside the fire.

"The men in the village told us where we could find you," explained Clovis.

"How are the villagers?" asked Marcus, his voice low so the children would not hear.

"Very well, actually," said Tristan. "I'm sorry to say that most of the casualties were among the Agorans."

"The good news is that there are even more Hestorians to cremate," interjected Zody.

Tristan continued. "We were sent to fetch the families of the dead so they could pay their respects to their sons and fathers."

"And Kaië, the young woman I had you follow, how is she?" asked Marcus, not wanting to appear overly concerned.

"Actually," said Zody, "she's right behind us."

Marcus turned his head toward the Fortress. The sun had risen above the trees now, and he saw a young woman running toward him.

"Kaië!" called Marcus. He felt elated to be in her presence once again

Kaië stopped at the fire, out of breath. She rested a moment before speaking. "I've come with a message. Lord Fredric requests the presence of Jayson and company. He wants to speak with Dokur's protectors."

"Jayson's gone down to the shore," Marcus told her. With a quick thanks, Kaië continued on through the grove toward the sea.

*   *   *

Kaië slowed her pace as she neared the edge of the grove. The new day was clear, and the cool air felt invigorating. She continued past the rocks toward the shore. Removing her sandals, she let her feet sink in the soft, fine sand.

Her stomach was taut with anticipation. Every day for fifteen years she had come to the sea in hopes of seeing Jayson's ship on the horizon. But instead of Jayson, the sea had brought war. But it was over now. Freedom was so near she could smell it on the breeze.

She found him sitting on a dune, his arms wrapped around his knees, gazing toward the horizon. On seeing him, Kaië caught her breath. Then she broke into sobs and fell on her knees.

"Master Jayson!" she cried.

Jayson turned to see who had called his name. He immediately stood and went to her. Taking her by the shoulders, he gently lifted her to her feet. Then he brushed away her tears with his hand.

"Kaië," he said with the tenderness of a father. "My little Mouse, how you've grown."

Kaië embraced him. "I've waited so long," she said. "I can hardly believe you're real!"

"Believe it, for I *am* real. But this island brings me only sad memories. I'll be leaving as soon as I can acquire a ship."

"But I have a message for you," said Kaië, "from Lady Ivanore."

Jayson shook his head. "There is no need for that now. Ivanore is dead."

The words brought more tears to Kaië's eyes. "Somehow, I've known it for many years. But she made me promise to deliver her message, and so I shall."

"All right," said Jayson, too exhausted in body and spirit to argue. "What is your message?"

"Ivanore wanted you to come to her."

"Come to her where?"

"To the house of your father."

Jayson's expression grew melancholy. "I cannot go," he said, turning his face to the sea. "Not now."

Kaië understood Jayson's reluctance. He had lost everything, sacrificed everything that was dear to him. But hadn't she as well? Hadn't she given fifteen years of her life waiting for this moment? She would never be free as long as she was bound by her promise. Now that Jayson stood before her, she would not let anything or anyone stand between her and freedom.

"She was always kind to me," Kaië recalled wistfully. "I secretly called her mother. Sometimes she would tell me stories of something called freedom. I did not know what it meant, being as young as I was, but the thought of having it thrilled me just the same.

"When Ivanore left the Fortress that night so many years ago, I followed her in shadow. I wanted more than anything to escape, as well. When she discovered my presence, Ivanore embraced me. She told me through her tears that I could not follow. It was too dangerous. And though I clung to her skirt and pleaded with her to change her mind, she would not be swayed.

"'I must go alone,' she said. 'Stay here in the village. Tell no one who you are or what you have seen. When Jayson returns, tell him where to find me. Then you will be free.'"

Kaië's voice trailed off. A damp mist blew up from the sea, infusing the air with the scent of saltwater. She took

Jayson's hand in hers and lifted it to her face. The tears on her cheeks moistened his fingers. "I swore an oath to accept nothing less than your vow that you would go to her," she said. "I must fulfill my promise by receiving yours."

There was silence as Jayson studied the empty space in front of him. After several moments, his expression softened. "I give my word," he told Kaië. "I will go."

Sixty-four

hen Jayson and Kaië returned to the grove near the Fortress, Kelvin was awake and eating breakfast by the dying fire.

"How do you feel?" asked Jayson.

Kelvin stretched out his arms, leaning forward then sideways. "I'm better than ever before," he said, "thanks to Marcus."

Marcus poured a bucket of seawater over the coals. Kelvin's comments made him feel uncomfortable, yet he was glad his friend was alive. There was no need ever to tell him of the true sacrifice he had been willing to make.

"Kaië says we're to meet with Lord Fredric," said Marcus, averting attention from himself. "We'd better get going."

As Kaië led Marcus and the other boys toward the Fortress, Jayson took Kelvin by the arm, holding him back. "I think this belongs to you," he said, holding out Kelvin's pendant.

Kelvin took it and placed it around his neck. "Thank you," he said. "I didn't think I would live to see another day. I wanted Marcus to have it if I didn't." Kelvin hesitated as though he wanted to say something more. "I owe you an apology," he said finally.

"Apology? For what?"

"For doubting you. For distrusting you because you are—"

"Agoran." Jayson finished the sentence, and Kelvin lowered his gaze, ashamed. "No apology is needed, Kelvin. Trust and respect must be earned. I hope I have earned yours."

Kelvin looked up into Jayson's gray eyes and smiled. They continued walking toward the Fortress, though slowly and at some distance behind the others.

"Your shard of Celestine, do you know its history?" asked Jayson. "Other than that your mother gave it to you."

Kelvin shook his head.

"The woman who owned it was quite beautiful," continued Jayson. "Long ago her husband was forced to leave her, but they swore that one day they would find each other again. She took her Celestine pendant and broke it into two pieces, giving her husband one half and keeping the other half for herself."

While Jayson spoke, Kelvin held the fragment of Celestine in his hand and traced the jagged edges with his eyes. "That woman was my mother," he said. He looked up, searching Jayson's face for answers to questions that had plagued him for a lifetime. "How do you know so much about her?"

Jayson withdrew the smooth semicircle of Celestine from his pouch and held it up. "Because," he said, "she gave me the other half."

Sixty-five

The Fortress gate had been left unguarded except for one soldier. His armor was dull and splattered with mud, but his countenance was proud. When Marcus, Kelvin, and the others approached him, they were met with an enthusiastic greeting. "Welcome," said the guard. "Lord Fredric is expecting you."

He led them through the gate and up a wide flight of granite steps to a pair of arches as tall as three men. Marcus gazed up in wonder as they passed into a great hall floored in white marble. Their footsteps echoed against the walls decorated with ornate tapestries and oil canvases depicting royalty from eras gone by. They passed by the door to Fredric's council chambers and the passage to the prisons far below. The shattered door still lay in pieces on the floor.

The guard continued up a second stairway that curved its way around the perimeter of the room to the second floor. Two more guards stood at attention before a massive, intricately carved mahogany door, the same door Marcus and Kaië had gone through during their earlier escape. He scanned the floor for any sign of the key but found only a red smear of blood. Grief clutched at Marcus as he recalled how Bryn had given his life to save them.

The door swung open on enormous brass hinges. Beyond it lay a red plush carpet edged in gold embroidery. The guard bowed and waved his hand over the carpet, indicating that he wished Marcus and his companions to walk ahead of him. They found themselves in the cavernous throne room. Despite the present crowd, the room was bathed in silence.

They made their way down the carpeted path that led through the center of the room to where Lord Fredric stood waiting. Bedecked in his finest robes, Fredric looked magnificent, just the way Marcus imagined a ruler should. However, Marcus still wished he were already back home in the fields of Quendel.

When they reached the throne, Jayson knelt on one knee. Marcus and the others followed his example.

Fredric motioned for them to rise. "Please, it is I who should be honoring you, and so I shall." Fredric snapped his fingers and a guard came forward, bearing a shallow wooden chest in his arms. "For coming to the aid of Dokur and for placing the lives of my people ahead of your own, I bestow upon you, Jayson of Agora, and those who accompany you, a treasure of immeasurable worth."

The guard unlatched the chest and lifted the lid. A collective gasp rose from the crowd. There, bedded in black velvet, were seven faceted Celestine stones each mounted in a silver ring.

"These gemstones are worth a small fortune," continued Fredric. "Few can afford to buy such treasures. But their value is nothing compared to the gift that you have given Dokur. Thus I, along with the entire realm, honor you."

The crowd broke into raucous applause and cheering. Fredric held up his hand to regain silence.

"For the Cyclopes and Agorans who showed such sacrifice and courage on our behalf, I cannot think of a better way to show my gratitude than to give you my solemn pledge to grant them their freedom and to reinstate to them ownership of the land of their forefathers."

Again the crowd cheered. When the cheering subsided, Jayson, visibly moved by Fredric's homage, asked permission to speak. Fredric nodded.

"My Lord," he began, "long have I been separated from the land of my birth. Not a day has passed that I have not thought of it and of the family I left behind. I had hoped, upon my return, to be reunited with my wife, your beloved daughter Ivanore. However," and here the emotion he felt threatened to overwhelm him, "I have learned such hope is futile since my beloved lives no more."

On hearing this news, Fredric bowed his head. Though he had long suspected that his daughter was dead, the finality of it sent a cold chill through his heart.

"The sorrow I feel is beyond expression," continued Jayson. "Yet it is with great joy that I announce that I have found my son."

A hush swept through the room like the receding tide. Jayson reached for the boy standing to his left. "Lord Fredric, I present to you the son of Ivanore, your grandson, Kelvin Archer of Quendel."

The crowd gasped in surprise. From the corner of his eye, Marcus saw the look of disbelief on Clovis's and the other boys' faces. Kaië was so happy she nearly burst into tears.

A cry of protest resonated through the room. Chancellor Prost approached the throne and wagged a bony finger in Kelvin's face. "Impossible!" he yelled. "This boy is an imposter! If Ivanore is dead, her child must be dead as well!"

"Kelvin *is* our son!" Jayson contended.

"To say this boy is Ivanore's son is to lay claim to Lord Fredric's throne and the control of the entire realm! There must be evidence, testimony."

"You want evidence?" replied Jayson. "Here it is, then."

He reached into his pouch. "Fifteen years ago Ivanore broke her seal and gave me half," he said, holding up his half-circle of Ivanore's Celestine medallion. Then Kelvin removed his pendant and held it up, as well. Jayson continued. "The boy has carried this shard with him his entire life."

"Where did you get that?" shouted Prost.

"It was my mother's," Kelvin answered, "my mother, Lady Ivanore."

Jayson placed the two pieces together. The fit was perfect. Only a small section of the seal was still missing. Yet Prost's anger only intensified.

"Fredric," he cautioned with a severe gaze. "You once vowed no half-breed would rule this land! You swore on your very life that this child would never live to be heir! Say the word, and I will have the guards seize him!"

"Silence!" Fredric shouted at Prost. "Fifteen years ago I heeded your advice to exile Jayson and my only son! That decision has brought me only misery and regret. I will hear no more of your counsel today!"

Prost ground his teeth in anger but said no more.

Fredric rose from his throne and stepped forward. Marcus noticed that his lips trembled and his eyes were moist with tears. Fredric took Kelvin and embraced him, weeping as he did so. "My boy," he cried, "my beloved grandson!"

Sixty-six

When the ceremony ended, Marcus and the other boys followed Jayson to the courtyard. Preparations had been made for their return trip to Quendel. They were given fresh horses, plentiful food, and warm blankets. Marcus looked forward to seeing Zyll again and to getting back to his studies. He wondered, too, what awaited him and the others there. Would they all receive the same reward? There was only one Rock of Ivanore, and it rightfully belonged to Kelvin. Surely, though, all their efforts would be given due recognition. Marcus decided not to trouble himself about that now. He was too anxious to be on his way home.

Fredric accompanied them to the outer gate. "You are my only heir," he said to Kelvin. "Won't you stay with me until the time comes for you take my place as king?"

Kelvin embraced his grandfather once again. "I will gladly stay with you, but first I must finish my quest," he said. "My friends and I have been given the charge of bringing the Rock of Ivanore back to Quendel."

"Why not let the others deliver it for you?"

Kelvin looked around him and smiled at Marcus and the other boys who stood beside him. "We—all of us—began this quest together. We will finish it together." He turned back to Fredric and bowed his head respectfully. "But I promise to return in the spring."

"If that is your desire," replied Fredric, "then I am a happy man, indeed."

The horses were brought to the gate with packs secured to their saddles. Marcus's horse was a white mare, sleek and lively. He stroked her nose. It was softer than anything he had ever felt before.

"She's a beauty," said Jayson from the back of a chestnut mount. "As fine as any I've seen. What will you call her?"

"I haven't decided," replied Marcus. "I just can't settle on the right name."

"It will come to you." Jayson circled his horse. "I suppose you'll be going back to complete your apprenticeship with Master Zyll."

"That is my plan."

"Well, seeing as I gave my word to accompany you, I suppose I'll have to come along. You don't mind, do you?"

Marcus smiled. "Not at all," he said. "Not at all."

Kelvin and the other boys had, by now, mounted their

horses and called to Marcus to join them. Before he left, however, he wanted to say goodbye to Kaië. He was glad to see her walking toward him.

"I meant to bring you this," she said. "You left it at the tavern." She held out a limp leather sack. Before Marcus could accept it, Jayson snatched it away. "Haven't you put this thing out of its misery yet?" he asked, laughing. He tossed it to Marcus, who examined it. To Marcus's amazement, Zyll's makeshift strap was still intact.

"I don't know," he said. "I kind of like it."

Jayson cleared his throat and nodded toward Kaië. Marcus felt his face flush.

"I'll think of you often," said Kaië. Her words warmed Marcus to the very core.

"Do you have to stay here?" he asked. "You could come to Quendel with us."

Kaië smiled at the invitation. "Maybe one day my journeys will bring me to the Jeweled Mountains. I would like to visit the son of Ivanore—and his friends. In the meantime, I will help my people repair their city."

Though Marcus felt disappointed, he understood her reasons for staying behind. He struggled to find the right words to express how he would miss her and how much he appreciated all she had done to help him. He could think of nothing adequate, so he simply reached out his hand to her. She took it. Her hand felt warm and soft in his.

A loud screech broke the silence between them. Xerxes rolled his eyes and hung his beak in a mocking expression.

"Such eloquence!" he said. "Tell her she is the most beautiful woman you've ever seen! Tell her you hope she stays well. Tell her something! Anything!"

"I'll name my horse after you," blurted Marcus before he could stop himself. Kaïë's eyebrows rose, and a bemused grin appeared on her face.

"Thank you," she said. "I am honored, truly."

"Brilliant," said Xerxes with noted sarcasm. "Simply brilliant."

Marcus was glad when Kelvin's horse left the gate accompanied by Tristan's, Zody's, and finally Clovis's. As he followed them through it, something glinted in the sun. He found a key hanging from the post. Marcus took it, turning it over in his palm. It was an ordinary iron key worn smooth in spots—Zyll's key! When he dropped it in the Fortress, he thought it lost forever. Yet someone had recovered it and left it here for him to find. But who?

Beyond the Fortress gates, a crowd had gathered to bid farewell to Dokur's heroes. Marcus caught a glimpse of a familiar face among them, a young boy with amber eyes. A moment later the boy was gone. Marcus smiled to himself. Somehow Bryn had survived, and Marcus hoped their paths would again cross one day.

The elation he felt at that moment made him want to run as fast and as far as he could. He snapped the reins and galloped ahead to catch up with the others. Soon Dokur would be far behind him. He was on his way home.

Sixty-seven

When Marcus and the others emerged through the border of the Black Forest, they were greeted with cries of, "They've returned! The boys have come home!" Young and old ran from their cottages into the streets of Quendel to greet the town's newest heroes. Kelvin led the parade of horses and riders through the center of town to the square where a large crowd was already beginning to gather. Tables were erected, and a feast was prepared. All were joyful and begged the travelers to relate their tales of adventure, which they willingly did.

Each boy soon had his own throng of admirers about him, ever eager for one more story. The young ladies of the village wore garlands in their hair and vied for their attention. Marcus marveled that only days earlier he was nothing more than an orphan apprentice, but now he was as a victor come back from war. He liked this attention very much but knew that not everyone felt the way he did.

He strained his neck to see over the heads of those gathered around him. There, sitting on his horse well away from the crowds and celebration, was Jayson. He had traveled with them to Quendel, but now that he was here, he looked as though he regretted his decision. When he turned his horse as if to leave, Marcus shouted out to him and made his way through the throng of people.

"Don't leave," he pleaded. "You've come so far with us, you must stay for a while. The celebration will be over soon, and then Kelvin will present the Rock of Ivanore to Master Zyll. You will be my guest."

Jayson agreed, promising to meet him at the enchanter's cottage at sundown.

The afternoon flew swiftly by, and soon night fell upon Quendel. The girl who had tearfully kissed Tristan on the day of their departure kissed him again. Both he and Zody were welcomed home by their families. Clovis presented his father with his crossbow still in good condition. They learned that the coward, Jerrid Zwelger, had returned to Quendel days earlier but had received no hero's welcome. He was given instead the task of thresher in the mill—and he was content to take it.

At sundown, Kelvin and Marcus met Jayson at Zyll's door. Zyll, who had shied away from the festivities due to the onset of a slight illness, was slow to answer the knock.

As the door to the cottage opened, Marcus greeted the old man with a warm embrace.

Zyll patted the boy's head fondly, welcoming him home. "So, you've returned," he said. "Was Xerxes a good companion for you?"

Xerxes ruffled his feathers and yawned. "I watched over the boy like a hawk," he said. "And it's a good thing, too. Without me who knows what mischief he might have gotten into!"

"Thank you for your guidance, my old friend," said Zyll, taking the walking stick from Marcus and leaning it against the inside wall. "And Kelvin, my boy! How are you?"

"A bit road-weary," answered Kelvin, "but overall I am fine, thank you."

"Well, come in the both of you," Zyll said, motioning them inside. "I've some hot porridge waiting on the table."

"Just a moment, Master," said Marcus, barely able to mask his excitement. "I've brought a guest."

Jayson stepped up to the door. The old man looked the visitor up and down but said nothing. His expression was that of utter astonishment. Marcus was concerned that perhaps Zyll felt his home was not suitable for guests and tried to think of a way to politely excuse him of this unexpected duty. But to his surprise Zyll held out his hands to Jayson, who took them in his own.

Jayson's icy expression melted as he spoke. "Hello, Father," he said.

Sixty-eight

Zyll was so overcome with emotion that he could not speak for some time. Finally, when he had gathered his wits about him, he invited Jayson and the boys inside.

"I knew you would come," Zyll said to Jayson. "Though we've been apart since you were a boy, I've watched you over the years in my divining bowl—a father's devotion, I suppose."

Jayson smiled and laid his hand on Zyll's. "At first I came only because of a promise," he said, "but now that I'm here, I'm glad I came."

Jayson sat at the table and graciously accepted a bowl of porridge.

Marcus, who was too much in shock to eat, could hold his tongue no longer. "Would someone please explain what is going on?" he demanded.

"You've had a long journey," said Zyll calmly. "Have some supper, and then we'll talk."

"I don't want supper," replied Marcus impatiently. "I want to know why Jayson didn't tell me you were his father."

Kelvin, who had remained silent until now, spoke up as well, though he sounded more hurt than surprised. "And I want to know why Zyll never told me he was my grandfather."

Zyll slid one bowl across the table toward Marcus and another toward Kelvin. "All your questions will be answered," he said, "but first you must eat."

Marcus and Kelvin reluctantly sat down and began their modest meal together before an inviting fire. As they ate, Zyll leaned his elbows on the table and laced his fingers together.

"Tell me, have you succeeded in your quest?"

"Yes," Marcus replied. "We've brought you the Rock of Ivanore."

"You discovered its true character, then?"

"It is two things, actually. The first is Jayson, Ivanore's husband, but you must have already known that."

"The second is this," added Kelvin, removing his pendant and laying it on the table. On this signal, Jayson emptied his pouch. His part of Ivanore's seal lay alongside Kelvin's. Zyll pushed the two pieces together with his forefinger.

"The Rock of Ivanore, her royal seal crafted of the finest Celestine. Where did you find it?"

Marcus related the story of how Jayson had come into his company and how it had been discovered that Kelvin was the son of Jayson and Ivanore, the heir to Lord Fredric of Dokur. Through the entire story Zyll sat in his chair, silent and thoughtful. After all was told, Marcus sat back to catch his breath.

"And what about the key?" asked Zyll. Marcus had failed to mention the key, and now he hesitated to answer.

"I did as you instructed," he said. "I used the key to practice my magic. I did improve my skills somewhat, though I admit its power was difficult to control. And then I lost it."

"*Lost* it?" replied Zyll, his eyebrows raised.

"I got the key back," added Marcus quickly. "But something happened while it was lost that I can't explain. I performed magic on organic matter."

"What sort of magic?"

Marcus cast a wary glance at Kelvin. Sensing Marcus's uneasiness, Kelvin spoke up.

"He healed me," he said. "I was told later that I was dead, and Marcus revived me."

"This is true," added Jayson.

A look of concern crossed Zyll's face. "Dead, you say? And Marcus, you have no ill effects from the experience?"

Marcus shook his head. "Not really," he replied. "I do have a little pain from the wound Arik gave me. But I'm sure I'll recover quickly."

Zyll scratched at his chin for a moment, deep in thought. "I am glad you are all right," he said finally. "Few would even attempt what you did—let alone succeed."

"But *how* did I do it? I didn't have the key!"

"Well, that is easy to explain," said Zyll, a sly smile creeping across his lips. "The key bears no magic."

"What?"

"I never said it did. What I said is that it would unlock your destiny. If you misunderstood me, that was your mistake."

"But Xerxes told me it was forged in the depths of Voltana!"

"And so it was . . . by a locksmith in the village there."

"But . . . but the magic . . . " stammered Marcus.

"The magic came from within you. You obviously had confidence in the key, which translated into confidence in your own abilities. When your confidence was strong enough, no key or any other crutch was necessary. And it seems that your abilities are far stronger than you or I ever imagined. Now, if I may . . . "

Marcus reached into his pocket. Withdrawing the key one last time, he laid it in his master's outstretched palm. Zyll went to the bookshelf and took down the wooden chest he had opened on the first day of the quest. He turned the key in the lock and opened the lid.

"That stone you brought me is incomplete," he said. "There is a piece missing."

"But Master, we don't know where it is," said Marcus.

"Of course you don't, but you asked for answers, and

I suppose now is as good a time as any to give them." Zyll reached his hand into the chest and, as he had done before, withdrew an object wrapped in his fist. He held out his hand and opened his fingers. There, lying in his palm was a triangular shard of sea-colored stone, the missing piece of Ivanore's seal. He laid the shard on the table beside the others, forming a complete circle.

Marcus did not know what to say. What could this mean? And how had Zyll come by the missing piece? The expressions on Kelvin's and Jayson's faces seemed to ask the same questions.

As though reading their thoughts, Zyll explained. "When Jayson was exiled," he began, "Ivanore fled her father's wrath. He had threatened to kill her child, and so she sought the only person whom she could trust."

"Her husband's father," interjected Jayson.

Zyll nodded and continued. "Though you and I had been estranged for many years, she hoped I would shelter her, which I did, of course. By the time she reached me, however, she was very ill. She eventually passed from this earth, but not before I swore to her that I would conceal her offsprings' identities to protect them from Fredric."

"But if you were my grandfather, why did the Archers raise me?" said Kelvin.

"I would have taken you myself," replied Zyll, "but according to our law, orphans go to the highest bidder. I simply could not afford both children."

Jayson looked up in surprise. "*Both* children?"

"When Ivanore came to me she was with child."

"I know," said Jayson. "She had our son, Kelvin, with her."

"Yes," said Zyll, "she had Kelvin with her, but she died giving birth to a second son to whom she left this last shard of Celestine."

Marcus's eyes fell upon the seal now. The pale blue-green crystal glistened in the firelight. He laid his hand on it, encircling it with his fingers. He thought of the dream of the angel woman he had had after healing Kelvin. The woman had given him a shard of Celestine. He had assumed it was Kelvin's, but now he realized the shard in his dream was identical to the one Zyll had set before him.

Zyll's voice continued, his words settling in Marcus's heart like a ray of spring sunlight. The expression on Jayson's face revealed that he felt the same.

"I took the child," said Zyll, "and named him Marcus."

Energy coursed through Marcus's body. His arm surged with heat, and his hand grew so hot that the stone beneath it glowed red.

When the heat finally subsided, he removed his hand, dropping it heavily on the table from exhaustion. But his fatigue felt strangely satisfying. What he saw before him renewed his strength. Ivanore's seal no longer lay fragmented. Its rough edges were now smooth. The Rock of Ivanore was whole once more. Marcus Frye had unlocked his destiny after all.

Acknowledgements

When my oldest son was eight, he asked me to tell him a bedtime story—not read him a story, but make one up as I went along. Night after night, this story grew. In time, I started writing some of it down. And so *The Rock of Ivanore* was born.

This book is dedicated to my son, Marcum. If it weren't for him, I would never have even thought of it. But all my children have had a hand in it. Carissa, you're my right-hand man and most trusted critic. No one reads anything of mine until it passes your inspection. Stuart, thank you for being my biggest fan. Brennah and Jarett, you inspire me every day to be the best writer and mother I can possibly be.

My husband, to whom I've been married for nineteen years, is my rock. He puts up with my crazy ideas, the walls covered in sticky notes, endless hours and days and months and years of me living in my creative bubble while the dishes and laundry pile ever higher. Gonzalo, thank you for being my best friend and for working so hard to provide for our family—and for making *all* my dreams come true.

My sister-in-law, Dorine White, is my fellow writer-in-arms. She loves fantasy as much as I do and has encouraged me every step of the way. Thank you to my brother, Trevor, for marrying her and giving me the sister I always wanted.

I am so grateful for my high school English teachers & college professors who made me fall in love with literature and nurtured my budding talent—Thelma Chapman, Fran Kristoff, Carol Spector, and especially Elizabeth Rose, who has been a friend to me and an aunt to my children for all these years.

My parents, Ray & Cyndi White, believed in me long before anyone else ever did. From the time I was five years old when I wrote my first poem, Mom always told me what a good job I'd done, while Dad offered advice on how to improve my writing skills. I needed both Mom's unconditional support and Dad's gentle instruction to reach my potential. Dad's amazing stories inspired me to write my own, and Mom's motto "If someone else has done it, you can learn to do it, too," instilled in me the drive to never give up on my dreams.

Thank you to Peggy Tierney at Tanglewood Press for loving *The Rock of Ivanore* as much as I do and for making my dream a reality. A special thanks to Kathy Everts and Tristan Elwell for lending their artistic talents to this endeavor, and to Lisa Rojany Buccieri for her wonderful editing. Thanks to Lauren Wohl and Rebecca Grose for their marketing and publicity skills and the rest of the team at Tanglewood.

Finally, I give thanks to my Heavenly Father and his son Jesus Christ for their tender mercies and for placing such wonderful opportunities and people in my path. Everything I do is always for them.

Author Bio

 Laurisa White Reyes spent many years writing for newspapers and magazines before mustering enough courage to pursue her dream of writing novels. Aside from her obsession with books, she also loves musical theater and fantasizes about singing on Broadway (one dream she does not intend to pursue). She lives in Southern California with her husband, five children, four birds, three lizards, two fish and one dog.

Please visit her website www.laurisawhitereyes.com and her blog www.1000wrongs.blogspot.com.

Coming in 2013

THE LAST ENCHANTER

Book II of The Celestine Chronicles

ord Fredric, ruler of Dokur, stood in his private chambers, staring out the window toward the sea. Below him in the bay, the recently decimated navy was busy rebuilding its ships. The harsh sounds of the cutting and hammering of wood, the shouts of men, and even occasional laughter came to him on a crisp, salty breeze. Fredric breathed it in. He was satisfied with the Navy's progress and convinced all would be ready by winter's end. When the time was right, Dokur's ships and her crews would set sail for the mainland to exact vengeance on those who had invaded them only a few short months earlier. The attack had come without warning, the carefully calculated plan born of the worst kind of betrayal. Fredric's own son had led the Hestorians to these very shores, and Dokur had nearly fallen by their swords. Surely their enemy would expect retribution and would be preparing for the attack as well.

Fredric heard the door behind him open. The gentle clinking of crystal against silver was the only introduction the visitor needed.

"Is it time already?" Fredric asked without turning. "I would like a little wine to soothe my nerves before bed."

The attendant, a young dark-skinned man named Arnot, filled a goblet and handed it to his Lord with a slight bow. Fredric held the goblet between his ring-laden fingers and lifted it to his nostrils.

"From the local vineyard. A superb choice."

He downed the contents and then replaced the goblet on Arnot's tray.

"I fear I have grown too old for battle," said Fredric, crossing the room to his bed. "These eyes have witnessed too much bloodshed, too much suffering."

He held out his arms while Arnot removed his scarlet robe and replaced it with a linen nightshirt. Once Fredric was dressed, Arnot went to the bed and pulled back the coverlet.

"Your bed is prepared, my Lord."

Fredric stepped forward and rested his hands on the edge of the mattress. "My stomach," he said. "It bothers me so."

"Perhaps you should rest, sir," replied Arnot.

Fredric leaned against the bed, but he did not lie

down. He rubbed his stomach with his right hand. Then he raised it to his forehead where a sheath of perspiration had formed.

"I am not well tonight. Ah," he continued, sighing, "such is to be expected at my age."

Suddenly, Fredric clenched his teeth together and his hands balled into fists against the mattress. He groaned as his entire body began to tremble. Fredric seized the quilt in both fists and pulled with such force that the fabric tore. A moment later he dropped to his knees gasping for air.

"I am in pain," he managed to say in a desperate voice. "Fetch my physician!"

Arnot remained where he stood, his back against the colorful tapestry that hung ceiling to floor against the wall. He stared at Fredric with unsympathetic eyes.

"Arnot," called Fredric, reaching for the attendant with both hands. "Please! You must help me!"

A faint smile appeared on Arnot's lips—so faint that Fredric wondered if his eyes were playing tricks on him. When the attendant finally moved from his spot and crossed the room to the door, Fredric felt relieved that help would be found. He lay down on the floor, too weak now to lift himself into the bed.

"Tell my physician to hurry," he whispered. "Tell him I am very ill."

Arnot placed his hand on the door handle and looked back at Fredric. The smile on his lips was now unmistakable, and there was a definite look of pleasure in his face.

"You are not ill," he said coolly, as though the news were inconsequential. "You have been poisoned."

Then Arnot slipped through the door and shut it quietly and securely behind him.